Shelly Pratt is an Amazon, word-of-mouth, bestselling, self-published author who is also traditionally published with Pegasus under the Vanguard imprint in the UK, and, with a small publishing house in the United States of America.

Only starting her writing career in 2012, she has achieved exceptional reception selling e-books in the USA, publishing over eight books, all in different genres.

Shelly lives with her husband, two children, and Labrador, Scooby Doo, in northern New South Wales in Australia. Snow skiing is her other passion.

RUINED

Shelly Pratt

RUINED

Vanguard Press

VANGUARD PAPERBACK

© Copyright 2014
Shelly Pratt

A CIP catalogue record for this title is
available from the British Library.

ISBN: 978-1-84386-979-5

Vanguard Press is an imprint of
Pegasus Elliot Mackenzie Publishers Ltd.
www.pegasuspublishers.com

Originally published in 2013 as an e-book

This edition first published 2014

Vanguard Press
Sheraton House Castle Park
Cambridge England

Printed & Bound in Great Britain

For my children, Paris and Charlie. I love you both to the moon and back.

For my husband, Steven. Best friend, lover, fierce protector (me of you, of course) and *'the one'* who truly gets me – heart and soul. Thank you for believing in me, always.

Acknowledgements

A heartfelt thank you to Pegasus and the creative team involved for giving me the chance to fulfil my dream of publishing in my birthplace. Mind blown.

Thank you to my mother, Susan, who has always been my Mamma Bear until I grew old enough to boss her. You always made me believe that anything was possible, and for that, I'm grateful.

Thank you to my dad, Stewart, and Kimie. Life is what we make it and I'm forever grateful that you knew, even before I did, that I was capable of great things.

A big thank you to my sister, Nicole, for your sage advice – there had to be one sensible person in the family.

Thank you to my brother, Neil, for being my creative muse. Most of my books are inspired by you, and that is because you are the most interesting character. Two peas in a pod, you and I.

Most of all, thank you to the readers. Those of you who have touted my work are the ones who have given me the opportunity to do something I'm passionate about. I'm forever grateful for the chance to share my stories with the world.

Preface

We all have secrets. Some are just buried deeper than others. But they're there – hidden deep within. Mine I bury in that little red box people call a heart. Sometimes I wonder if I have a heart at all, for if I did I surely wouldn't do the things I've done. Some people have that line they just don't cross, while others have never had to draw it in the sand in the first place. They already know what is right from wrong. They know the consequence of stepping over it and they are just not willing. Others go barreling clean over it. No care for boundaries at all. Me, I know what ramifications my actions would have. Well, if anyone ever found out about them. But they won't. I will never tell a soul my secret. It will just be mine.

There are times I am on my own and I let my mind dwell on it. It rolls around my head consuming my thoughts and I have to admit I like it. Does this make me a bad person? Perhaps. I am willing to feel guilt over my deception because my actions cause me so much pleasure. These moments are only brief. I can't risk being found out. Too many people would be hurt.

So I live my life according to the rules of others while my secret festers its way through my body. It bleeds slowly out of my heart and into my veins. Each word of my secret pulsing through me as it gets closer to the surface. I imagine one day it will get so close to the surface it will spring forth from my lips and reveal the monster I really am. There would be a giggle and then a torrent of words. I envision people seeing the manic woman confessing her sins to the world and revealing the dark side that lurks beneath. It won't be pretty. The twisted faces of those who realize they've been deceived, and then the torture when they see me for who I really am.

So I prolong this day as long as possible, living my life with as much normalcy as I can. No one will know the real me.

No one will know that I have been willingly ruined by Angel – at least not while I can keep my mouth shut.

One

I live in Astoria, Oregon. It's a small town that boasts being the oldest American settlement established west of the Rocky Mountains. My favorite movie of all time, *The Goonies*, was filmed here when I was a child. But I'm an adult now, and have responsibilities and obligations.

My fiancé and I reside in a house on The North Slope. I bought it when I was just twenty-three with money I had inherited from my grandfather. When I was younger my family and I used to vacation here, and I fell in love with the place instantly. Having my own money allowed me to make the move from my home town of Washington DC. The Victorian home I purchased looks north towards the Columbia River and I wouldn't trade the high winds and rain that blanket the slope for anywhere else in the world.

Carron was working as a doctor at the local hospital when I needed stitches for a laceration to my arm. There were a lot of renovations to do on the house, and with money starting to dwindle I had taken upon doing them myself. It was silly really, but a simple slip on the wet driveway allowed the broken window I was carrying to slip and slice deeply into my arm. I bandaged it quickly and drove myself to the Columbia Memorial Hospital.

The minute I laid eyes on him I knew he was a kind man. He had warm hazel eyes that twinkled behind his glasses. I knew he was a lot older than me by the whispers of grey hair that graced his sideburns. He fixed my arm, and I wondered if he might be able to fix the rest of me too.

For a while, I didn't think I would ever be able to be with another man. Carron changed that. He pursued me relentlessly for six months until I said I would go out with him. At first I thought it would just be companionship. But he offered stability when all I had known was destruction and hopelessness. I gave myself to him in the only way I knew how – I slept with him. That was a year and a half ago.

Recently, Carron asked me to marry him. I said yes. Not because I'm in love with him – because I'm not. I do love him, though only as much as one can when they feel their soul is ultimately tied to another. It has always been this way since I was fifteen. I know my feelings will never change, so I have made the best of what I can. Life with Carron sometimes feels like a lie. Sometimes I feel like a rotten shit for keeping him around, especially when he looks at me with those eyes. Sad and soulful – willing me to give him more than I am capable of. But I will never be able to give him the love he deserves.

He never quits on me though. My life with him sometimes seems like one big apology, and I know he tries to figure out how to unlock the secrets of my heart. But to be honest, I'm sure if he ever did he would wish he'd never bothered because I know he will not like what he finds there.

I'm walking home from work. It's the middle of November and a chilly seven degrees out. The late afternoon sun is weak and watery and a cool breeze floats off the water. My hands are full of grocery bags with food to prepare a meal. We are having dinner tonight with friends – his friends. As with every aspect of my life, I am a reluctant participant in what I consider mundane socialization. Carron sees things completely differently, of course, but manages to hide his embarrassment and confusion at my lack of social graces quite well. I'm sure his friends think of me as snobby or standoffish, but the fact remains I just have no desire for friends. It only means more people I have to lie to and, sometimes, the guilt comes knocking pretty fucking loudly on my door.

I hurry up the hill, struggling to juggle all my grocery sacks. As I make the turn onto Seventeenth Street I am suddenly shocked into coming to an abrupt halt. As he drives by in a rental car, our eyes connect instantly. I've been longing to see him for so long and here he is, so unexpectedly real, driving out of the street I live on. Warmth spreads over his dark features and I remember what it is like to run my hands through his short brown hair while his hands caress my body. These thoughts of him are intoxicating. He stops the car, but does not get out. The urge to touch each other would be far too strong for both of us.

The engine of the car hums as exhaust fumes plume out the back. I want him to run to me – take me away with him and never look back. But he won't. He wants me to have a normal life, not one where we have to hide. It is a bitter pill to swallow – the fact that I have missed him calling in to see me unexpectedly. It doesn't happen often, but when it does I go into a complete meltdown. I become a junkie, willingly opening up for my fix and then completely falling apart when it is taken away again. Hi, my name's Bailey Michaels and I'm a sucker for punishment.

The thing is, though, I don't want normal. I only want him.

No, that's not even right.

I need him. I need Angel.

Like he always does, he leaves. I'm left standing like someone has just run a knife through my heart and I let out a little sob. It takes all my willpower not to drop to my knees and cry like a baby. I'm close, but by the skin of my teeth I manage to pull myself together before the tears start. No matter what my heart desires, I know he can never give it to me. The only problem we both have is learning to accept that fact once and for all.

The wind fiercely whips my long auburn hair across my freckled face and I snap back to reality. I curse when I realize how late it is getting and hurry up the street to my house before Carron gets home. I'm going to need time to compose myself so he doesn't suspect anything is amiss.

The Victorian house is full of character. I have put every bit of my soul into it and have lovingly restored it to its original glory. The outside is painted in a cream colored paint with black accents here and there. Steps that lead from the footpath to the front door have been painstakingly tiled with a mosaic pattern. It is original and unique which gives the whole house an eclectic feel. The side verandah affords views over the whole town and I will often sit in the rocking chair with my cat, just taking in the view. She greets me now as I climb the stairs, wrapping her tail around my ankles and almost tripping me as I go.

'Shoo, Jezebel.' She meows in response, but persists in her affectionate onslaught. Once inside she runs straight to the bay window to take up her position on the pillow that holds prime real estate next to pipes that carry hot water to heat the house. I ignore her as I head to the kitchen and dump the groceries on the bench. I'm eager to shower, hoping the water will wash away the tension of the shock at seeing Angel.

The water blasts out of the showerhead and I have it as hot as I can stand. I shampoo my hair, taking longer than usual to knead my fingers across my scalp and massage away the headache that is building. My thoughts drift to Angel and I wish that he could take all my pain away like he did in high school. He saved me that day. His arms were like a warm blanket around me when I was battered and bruised. Angel always tells me it was I who saved him, but I think he has it a little mixed up. Nobody gets me the way he does. The only problem is, there is no way in hell we can be together.

Not then, not now, not ever.

I am startled out of my reverie when the bathroom door abruptly opens.

'Hey, Bails, are you almost done in there honey?'

'Ah, yeah.'

'Okay, babe. Do you want me to start peeling the vegetables for tea?'

'That would be great; I'll be just a sec.' My tone belies my misery. I want to be a happy person for Carron, and for him to be happy with me. Lately, though, I've become unsure I can do this forever. He leaves me to finish up and goes back downstairs to start on dinner. By the time I join him in the kitchen he has diced all the vegetables and turned the oven on to preheat for the chicken I am going to roast.

'Thanks for doing the vegetables.' I kiss his cheek and am comforted by his scent. It is familiar and masculine.

'Anytime. I poured you a wine.' He nods to the glass on the end of the bench.

'Thanks; how was your day?' Carron's day varies between manageable and chaotic, depending on what our small town throws at him.

'My day was great actually,' he says as he puts the chicken into a roasting tray. 'I had a sweet little girl come in with a broken arm – she was very brave though.' He smiles at the memory.

'Must have been painful for her.'

'Yeah, but the promise of a lollipop made her putty in my hands. Made me think of what it would be like for us to have kids.' His voice trails off a little. He is wistful, but knows I have never really made plans for the future. Hell, I think when I said yes to his proposal he was more surprised than I.

'Mmm-hmm.' I busy myself with setting the table. He eyes me carefully; there is an undercurrent in the air that he can't ignore.

'Everything okay? How was your day?'

'It was all right. A little tiring, that's all.' I work for Danzar. It's a high-end fashion magazine that distributes out of Boston. Their head office is there, but they have staff working for them all over the country. We have a small office in town because I am lucky enough that there are four of us in the area who do contract work for them on a regular basis. We all obtained our positions through word of mouth. My best, and only girlfriend Lyra works there as a photographer, but even she doesn't know my secret. I'm also good friends with James who works in our office. He used to live next door to the house we vacationed in when I was little. We've stayed really close over the years.

Carron nods, willing to accept my response, but I'm not sure he is really buying it. A ring of the doorbell saves me from further explanation. I shove thoughts of Angel back down to the bottom of my heart and lock the door for the day. It is dangerous to start thinking of him when I am in the company of others.

Dinner is what it always is when Carron's colleagues come for a meal. All they talk about is medical shit that I find completely boring. I drink too much red wine to pass the time and smile and nod at intermittent points in their conversation. Scott and Leila are a husband and wife team who work the pediatric ward in the hospital. They're a little older than Carron who is already a good seven years older than me at thirty-three. I'm sure it is just in my head, but I always feel that his friends who are older than me tend to look down on me.

Leila offers to help with dessert, although I politely refuse. I'm going to sneak a quick cigarette out on the back patio and don't want her hanging around. I clear the plates to take with me and dump them on the kitchen bench. While I warm some ready-made fudge in the microwave, I sneak out the side door to have my fix. This is not a regular habit, but one I indulge in when I have had too many drinks. The nicotine goes straight to my head and the ground spins before me. Being drunk takes the edge off my day. My mind flits from one thought to the next, which is great because I don't really want to focus on *him*. I'm startled when the door opens and the warmth from inside spills out into the frigid air.

'I thought I'd find you out here.' Carron slinks in behind me and wraps his arms around my waist. The guilt creeps up. *Yeah, just add it to the list*, my subconscious yells at me.

'Sorry,' I say as I take the last drag and exhale into the black sky.

'Those things will kill you, you know.' It's his standard doctor line every time he catches me out. I respond the same way I always do.

'Not today they won't.' He chuckles. He knows he won't win this argument with me – it's just a verbal dance we always do. I like that he respects me enough to let me do what I want to do.

'Don't be too long,' he admonishes, kissing the back of my head. 'Our guests are waiting for dessert.'

'Coming now.' The cigarette is ground out and I follow him back into the kitchen. Dessert is plated up and Carron helps me serve it to our guests. He slips me a strong black coffee, attuned to the fact my speech is a little slurred and movements a little slow. Thankfully the rest of the evening goes by rather quickly. They're all on the a.m. shift, so they leave us not long after the clock strikes 9:00 p.m. The dishes are left where they sit because I promise to do them first thing in the morning. Carron doesn't argue because he is eager to get to bed. But I find out it is not for sleep, but sex.

The deed is always missionary position between the two of us. Since day one Carron observes the unwritten rule never to expect anything else. The truth is, I am one kinky bitch – just not with him because it reminds me too much of being with Angel. So I stick to safe sex positions where my mind doesn't wander to my lover who took my virginity.

Carron and I always do it in the dark. This way I don't have to look into his face and feel like I am betraying anyone. It's just a physical need we both get to satisfy. I know he deserves more, but I am selfish enough to recognize I keep him around because I am unbearably lonely. Unfair, I know, but he has told me he's not going anywhere. To be honest I think he thinks I am damaged goods and takes pity, but for the life of him I'm sure he can't figure out how I got to be this way.

We do the routine stuff like brush our teeth and use the toilet before sliding into bed together. It's cold and I am glad for the warmth of his body. I snuggle up next to him and breathe in his scent. My body relaxes and I wait for him to make the first move. It is always him who does.

He rolls onto his side and slides his hands over my hips. His warm, large hands grip me tightly, bringing me closer to him. His fingers trail up my waist and past my ribcage to my breasts. As his lips cup my mouth and softly kiss me, his hand starts to rub my nipples. I let my tongue trail over his lips, the sensation sending a sigh from his mouth. His breath is minty and tickles my cheek. Carron reaches for my night shorts and tugs them gently down towards my ankles. I don't wear any panties underneath. What's the point when I know they will only come off?

He lies down on top of me and I can feel his erection press firmly against my thighs as he makes his way back up to the top. There are never clothes on his body for bedtime, no matter what the weather is like. My top is left on, because he knows I hate feeling cold. That is Carron all over; self-sacrificing to put my needs first.

We continue to kiss. His mouth is urgent and I struggle in my alcohol haze to focus on the present. My mind lingers to this afternoon and the sight of Angel stubbornly refuses to leave my thoughts. While Carron is making love to my body, in my head Angel is making love to my soul. With him occupying my thoughts, my body starts to act accordingly. I'm suddenly needy for touch. My arms wrap around Carron's neck and I pull him eagerly on top of me. Our tongues clash against each other's and I fight for breath as his touch draws me in. I buck my hips to meet his and his cock probes my sex, gently asking for permission to be inside of me. My legs part wider, granting him access to my wet depths.

He moans as he slides inside of me and I wrap my legs around his waist to hold him there. The pressure is just enough to keep me wanting more. We gently rock back and forth. He touches me and rubs me consistently so that I will definitely orgasm. His tempo increases the more I pull on his arms and I feel his need spread through his body. Not once has he ever come before me. Pleasing me is his first priority and then he quickly rushes to finish. That is what I like about Carron's nature; he makes others happy before himself. Tonight is no different. I come all over him and he lets out a satisfied grunt as he continues to thrust deep inside of me, searching for the release he is looking for. With a final push he comes, semen seeping from his cock as he stills and lets his body pulse with pleasure. We are both panting as he rolls off and lays spent on his back.

I go to the toilet and expel the evidence of our love making. When I join him back in bed, he slings an arm over me and drifts off to sleep easily. Soon, contented snores drift from his side of the bed. While he sleeps my mind wanders to Angel. I don't normally allow myself to think of him when Carron is around, because I know it will only end in tears. But the unexpectedness of seeing him today has me rattled. I wonder what it was he was doing here. He was here to see me, but why? What would he have said? What would he have done? Exhaustion finally takes over my body. The last thing I remember before I fall asleep is a single tear trickling down my face as the bedroom ceiling leaves my vision.

Two

Work the next day brings a mixed bag of feelings. I'm horribly grumpy because my hangover is taking its toll by half past ten. But by 11:00 a.m. I am just about walking on cloud nine. This is all due to the email I have just received. The New York office has an assignment for me and they have asked if I am able to fly out there next week.

I eagerly type my response, which is 'Hell yeah!' Don't get me wrong, it is not the excitement of the trip that thrills me. It is the prospect that I may get to see Angel. Work requires me to travel quite frequently, and it is while I'm away that I hope to meet up with Angel. He doesn't always say yes. In fact he tries to stay well away from me. But the pull of being together never keeps us apart for too long. Even he is not that strong, despite his belief that he's bad for me. Bad for us.

I send a quick text to Carron, just letting him know I will be out of town from Monday through Thursday of next week. A short while later his message back lets me know that it will not be a problem. My mind thinks that if I am at least honest with him about my whereabouts and what I am working on then there will be no excuse not to trust me. The receptionist out of the New York office sends an email to say she will book my airline ticket once she receives confirmation that I have accepted the assignment. I get right on it, afraid that if I take too long they will assign the job to someone else. The next thing I am about to do sends a thrill through me and I need to take a steadying breath before I compose the email.

To: thurmontlumberyard@wizzmail.net
From: bails@quickmail.com
Subject: Trip to NY
Dear Angel
I find myself in NY on business from Monday through Thursday next week. Available? Bails xx

There is no response for a while. He normally doesn't reply quickly. I know he will be thinking very carefully as to whether he should join me or not. He tries with every fiber in his body to stay away but, like me, sometimes the drug is just too strong. I know he will have no trouble leaving work for a couple of days. He has his own lumber business in Maryland, just north of Washington in a little town called Thurmont. Usually he's able to leave it running in the capable hands of his foreman if he needs to get away.

Giving up after half an hour, I shut down my computer so I can go and get some lunch. There is a little coffee shop just a block away from the office and they have a soup and pasta menu that changes daily so the locals don't get bored. When I get there the smells from the kitchen seep out from the entryway and my stomach starts to growl in response. I skipped breakfast this morning as I felt far too queasy to face food, but now I am ravenously drooling at the counter.

The owners, a couple of old timers who have lived in Astoria since day dot, run the shop together. The woman does all the cooking while the husband serves at the front counter. His name is Ben and he always offers a kind smile from underneath his bushy moustache. He is a big round fellow who looks like he indulges in far too many of his Mrs' goodies. Today they have pumpkin soup with sour cream and he serves me an extra-large portion. Ben winks at me when he passes it to me and tells me I need to put some weight on. It is our routine where he always insists I need more meat on my bones, but I rebuke him that his efforts are in vain because you can't fatten a thoroughbred. I pay him the flat five-dollar fee and wave as I leave the store.

I practically run into Carron as I step onto the sidewalk. That's the problem with working in a small town. Everybody sees everybody if they're out and about. I forgot he had his early start and would be looking for his lunch about now. He catches me before I bump into him and steadies me with his strong arms.

'Hey there, you're looking mighty happy this morning.' His smile is warm and inviting and I feel bad that it is not him who evoked these emotions from me.

'Aren't I always happy?' I sulk when he says things like this, partially because it is rare that I am ever completely and utterly happy.

He cups my chin and leans forward to kiss my cheek.

'Don't sulk, I'm only teasing you! I can't stop and chat, I have a limited time before my break is over and the ER has been crazy today. How about we go out for dinner tonight?'

'That would be great. How about you pick me up from work around six?'

'Sure. I'll duck home and have a shower and feed Jezebel before I come get you, okay?'

'Great, I'll catch you then,' and hurry off before he has time to comment on my mood any further.

I make it back to the office without slopping any of the soup out of its container and sit my ass down at my desk to eat it. Its warmth slides down my throat and heats the center of my belly. I feel much better now I am getting food into me – not nearly as queasy as this morning. Instead of a hangover I'm now bubbling with hope that I won't be alone in New York.

I boot the computer back up, butterflies fluttering around in my stomach and a giddy feeling washes over me. My email springs to life and shows three new messages in my inbox. The first is from him.

To: bails@quickmail.com
From: thurmontlumberyard@wizzmail.net
Subject: Trip to NY
Dear Bailey,
I'm coming. Please advise hotel.
Angel.

I want to jump out of my chair and dance and scream because I am so filled with elation. But I don't. Instead I sit calmly and hit reply on his email.

To: thurmontlumberyard@wizzmail.net

When I press send I feel a little guilty that I will be leaving Carron and spending time with another man. But I can't help it. I want him. I *need* him. He is the one person who I will ruin everything else good in my life for, despite how bad he thinks our relationship is.

The rest of the day is spent in a blur, my haze of happiness making the time go a lot quicker. James is the only guy who works with us here in Astoria and he usually organizes the layout of the magazine's pages. Lyra is our in-house photographer. Jenna and I are the writers and usually do all the interviews for the magazine on the north-west coast. I love my job. Sometimes it seems like the only place I can really be me.

I offer to stay back this evening as I have already made plans with Carron to go out for dinner. The others leave by ten past five, so it is only a short while on my own until he gets here.

Most of my work is up to date, so I allow myself time to read a little. I've been reading *One Flew Over The Cuckoo's Nest* by Ken Kesey. I'm not yet finished, but feel the characters have traits I possess. Devious, wicked and a little mad, with sanity clearly evading some of the characters altogether – I find the story quite genius.

In my peripheral vision I notice movement on the curb outside the office. The big arch windows allow a full view of the street and I see Carron has just parked his car and gotten out. It has turned dark outside, with the rain clouds threatening the sky and hanging low over the hillside. The street lights have come on and he sees me sitting by the light of my desk lamp. I wave and make to collect my belongings before shutting off the lights and heading for the door. He's waiting at the front door for me and I offer him a kiss on his freshly shaved face. He smells good; the aftershave I bought him for his birthday lingers on the sweater he's wearing. I set the alarm and lock the door.

'Ready?' he confirms.

'Yep, where are we off to?'

'I thought we'd go to Mimishkins.' His eyes gleam in delight. He knows this is my favorite restaurant and my mouth starts watering in anticipation. Mimishkins is a new Italian restaurant that has opened up down on Pier 39 where the popular restaurants are located. He helps me with my coat and opens the car door for me. We head east on Columbia River Highway and enjoy a comfortable silence while Ed Sheeran's *Drunk* plays on the stereo. *How apt.*

The restaurant is close, so it doesn't take us long to get there. Carron easily finds a park as it's midweek and not the season for tourists to be visiting. I wrap my coat a little tighter around me as I get out of the car and step into the cool breeze. If the temperature drops much lower than this we may very well have snow. My nose tends to sniff out when the change is coming.

Carron comes around my side of the car and offers his arm.

'Why thank you, kind sir.'

'Most welcome, ma'am.' The sides of his eyes crinkle at our banter and I'm glad he's such a carefree person. He's the complete opposite of Angel, which is maybe why I was drawn to him in the first place. He's not as intense, instead being chilled and unaffected by most things. It takes a lot to faze Carron and I think this is why he is so good at his job.

The restaurant is beautiful and affords views right out onto the bay. The hostess leads us to a table right next to a big window, the lights of nearby establishments twinkling in the distance. I love the fact that the entire restaurant is lit with candles; it makes the ambience warm and inviting.

We sit comfortably in a corner nook and snuggle in side by side. I prefer this, because I feel that if we sit facing each other then there is nowhere else to look but each other's face. This makes me uncomfortable at the best of times, but especially when I'm about to be lying my ass off to my fiancé. I mean really, I'd rather not get caught out in a lie and sometimes I feel that Carron looks at me far too intently for his own good.

A wine list is produced and Carron selects a bottle of chilled Semillon Blanc. We order entrées and mains; the waitress thanking us for our order before leaving us be.

'So, off to New York hey?' Carron raises his glass in a toast and I clink it softly with his.

'Yeah, it's going to be pretty cold this time of year though, and let's not forget extremely busy with all the shopping people will be doing in the lead up to Christmas.'

'Oh, it won't be too bad. Just take a taxi everywhere.'

'You can count on it – there is no way I'm getting a car. Doesn't matter how many times I go there I still cannot find my way around the city – it's too big and busy.'

'Well maybe I should come with you and I could show you around when you have some time off.' I just about spit my sip of wine out in his face and struggle to maintain my composure as I swallow the mouthful.

'It probably wouldn't be any fun for you, Carron. I mean, I'm only going for three and a bit days and really will be spending a lot of time in meetings. The other staff and I will probably just end up grabbing takeout for our meals. I seriously doubt you would have any fun at all.' I hope my first lie of the evening is a convincing one.

'That wouldn't bother me at all, Bails. I'm sure you could excuse yourself for meals – you're going to need a break at some stage, aren't you?'

'Sure, but then I will probably just be catching up on sleep. We'll be keeping pretty long hours.' *Lie number two, done and dusted.*

'Are you sure, aren't you gonna miss me?'

'Of course I will. But it really isn't necessary. Besides, you've already booked your time off with the hospital for Christmas. They probably would be too short staffed to allow you to just duck off for a short break.' *Way to go, Bailey, make him feel guilty about his patients so he won't interfere in your affair.*

'I suppose you're right, I just thought it would be nice for the two of us to get away together.'

'Me too, but perhaps another time when it isn't just on a whim, okay? Maybe we can plan a trip just the two of us after Christmas?'

'I'd like that.' We are interrupted by our entrée and Carron's mood has come down several notches. I'm feeling guilty as sin right now, but despite how lousy I feel at rebuking his suggestion, there is nothing that will make me feel bad enough to make me want to cancel my plans with Angel. I take several sips of my wine and do what I always do when I have made him miserable – indulge him with affection.

My hand reaches for his under the table and he smiles begrudgingly as I stroke his fingers with my own. He takes a sip of his wine and I offer him an oyster with my fork. His lips part and he waits while I place it on his tongue. There are questions not asked that linger in his eyes and I can't bear to look into them anymore, so busy myself with breaking bread and chatting about random stuff like the weather and politics. To be honest, I don't give a fuck about either, but it beats the hell out of having to cut the air with a knife. I'll stick with the small talk to keep him from discussing my job. Or New York.

When we've finished I settle the bill and leave a tip. It's getting late and we both have work tomorrow so we decide to have coffee at home. By the time we pull into the carport it's gone 9:00 p.m. The phone is ringing loudly when we enter through the kitchen and Carron rushes to grab the receiver.

Three

'Hello, Doctor Fields speaking.' I can tell by Carron's side of the conversation that he's going to have to head back to Emergency. I flick off my shoes and turn on the kettle so I can make a cup of tea for myself and a thermos of coffee for Carron. Considering the day he's had, it looks like he is going to need all the caffeine he can get.

'Bad news?' I ask when he disconnects the call.

'There's been a two car accident on the hill. It looks like a huge transport vehicle has been involved and a family with young kids. I think reports this early from response teams have said icy conditions have been a factor. Looks like I'm in for a few hours' work until they get things under control in the ER.'

'God, it sounds serious. Do you want me to drop you down there?' I hand him his thermos of coffee, concern etched on my face. He leans forward and strokes my cheek.

'Don't be silly. It's probably best if I take the car and then I can just come home whenever I finish. You go to bed, there's no point both of us doing without sleep.' Even though I'm tall Carron seems like a giant next to me, standing an impressive six foot three. I stand on tippy toes to kiss him briefly on the lips, but when I pull away he holds on tight and cups my chin in his hands.

'I love you, you know?' I swallow heavily, as I always do when he says this. There is nothing on this earth that makes me feel like a bigger shitheel than when he says those three little words. Probably because I know I am undeserving of them.

'I know you do. You be safe now okay?'

'Always.' He leaves me against the kitchen counter and Jezebel comes in through the cat door to take his place. Good old cat knows just when to stick around and the right time to fuck off again. She rubs around my ankles and I bend down to scratch between her ears.

'Looks like it's just you and me, puss.' She meows and follows me upstairs to the bedroom. I let her take up position on the end of the bed, knowing full well if Carron were here he'd have something to say about it. My book holds my attention for all of ten minutes before I feel my eyes start to close. The last dregs of my tea are cold so I rinse my mug in the bathroom and hop back into bed and turn the lights off.

While I am in that state of semi-consciousness and sleep I can feel the secrets in my chest. Slowly they move within my heart, the heart I keep locked. At first it is just a snippet… a word he said or a look. Pretty soon all manner of things are jumping and rattling around inside, almost like an incessant monster trying to get out from lock and key. Touches, kisses, promises, begging, pleading and abandonment – it's all there raging like a storm in my chest, unleashed for me to feel the full impact of what the memory of all those things mean.

'This is so fucked up!' I scream so loudly the cat jumps off the bed and bolts out of the room. I doubt she will be back anytime soon. Rolling onto my side I bang my fist into the pillow and sob.

'Why does it have to be wrong? Why, why, why!' My anger soon turns to a muffled wail as I cry myself to sleep. The only problem is that no matter how many times I sleep, I will never wake up in a world where loving Angel is okay. I will only ever be able to have him in the snippets he allows.

As darkness takes hold and I succumb to the dreams, calm takes over my body. He comes to me like this. In my head while I sleep. It's always safe. It's always exactly what I want it to be. Just me and him. Tonight I dream of the night of my high school graduation. He makes me go, so reluctantly I do. At first I shook my head. No, I really don't want to go I plead. In my dream my head-shaking is an exaggerated gesture. I almost giggle, realizing the scene resembles something more in keeping with the modern *Alice In Wonderland* flick.

'Why don't you want to go? You'll regret it you know. Every girl needs to go to a ball at least once in their life.' His adorable face smiles at me, but drifts away and fades as the dream takes me to another place.

I'm in the huge school hall. My dress is made with gorgeous blue silk that brings out the color in my eyes. Sequins have been hand-sewn into the strapless bodice, each one twinkling as the lights reflect off them. Our prom setting is very pretty – not at all like when it is used as the gymnasium. Lights dance on everybody's skin and music booms loudly while students drink punch and laugh. I try to make out who the students are, but every time they turn to look at me all I see is their blurry distorted face.

A few game ones have started to dance, and several couples have been broken apart already by faculty for making out on the dance floor. When the students separate, their bodies dissipate into a swirl of mist which floats across the room. I reach out my hand to touch it, wondering where they disappeared to, but the mist is cold and I retreat my hand back to my body.

There is no date here for me because, seriously, there is no way we can be seen together like that. But I know he is close. He knows I need him close. When my arrival is finally noticed I see the subtle change in the atmosphere. People start to whisper to each other. They talk. They have heard rumors about what happened to me, but never being told the truth leaves them to make up their own mind. I try to ignore them, but if I am honest, I am unsuccessful. Their obvious curiosity makes me want to bolt. But I can't. I promised. One song. I have to be here for at least one song. Whether I dance or not, he feels it is important for me to be here.

So I watch while I delicately sip on punch in a plastic cup. I almost make it. There's something about the air around me that suddenly makes me want to choke. I could blame it on the smoke machine that is providing atmosphere, but I'm sure it is the fact that a group of girls have just surrounded me.

'What the fuck were you thinking by coming here?' The ringleader always has so much to say. I bet she wouldn't feel so confident if her posse wasn't standing right behind her. I'm still afraid. Even after all this time. While I am dreaming, I wonder absently why my subconscious chooses to see these faces and not the others.

'I, ah…'

'She asked you a question, cunt.' The words are like acid as they spew from one of the follower's mouths.

Thankfully we are interrupted.

'Is there a problem here?' I turn to look, but by the voice I already know who it is. His forehead shows a very visible frown, his displeasure at the girls around me quite evident on his face. I'm instantly thankful that he has taken this opportunity to happen by. My eyes dart to his, and there is unspoken meaning that passes between us. He nods to me.

'Are you okay, Bailey?'

'Yes,' I mutter. He turns back to the girls, their obvious hatred for me still etched on their made-up faces.

'I asked you girls a question. Is there a problem here?'

'No, Coach Sawyer,' they reply.

'Well I suggest you all go back and enjoy the dance before you are asked to leave.' His tone is harsh and they look at him warily, not quite certain if he will follow through with his threat. They hold their ground for just a moment before clearing off. With the girls gone, he can do nothing but look at me.

'You okay, Bails?' Concern oozes from him. We both know this is not the time or place for this discussion.

'Sure, Mr. Sawyer,' I say loud enough for any big ears nearby who might be listening in.

'Well good. If you need me, I'll be close by.' He nods, and retreats to the teachers' table where they are supervising from the back of the hall. I watch him walk away. God I wish he would stay. I know he's worried about me, but this is not the time for him to be showing favoritism in front of other students. That will just earn me more flack than I need. Even so, I feel safer when he's by my side. The air starts to lack the oxygen I so desperately need. I need to get out of here.

While I'm sleeping, I know I am dreaming. But there is no way I want to wake up. The best part of the dream is yet to come. The bed shifts, and the sheets move. In my semi-conscious state, I realize it must be Carron, just home from the hospital. My body relaxes. Knowing I'm not in danger, I seek to head back into the recesses of my brain where I am certain my dreams will bring Angel back to me.

The stuffiness of the gymnasium is replaced by a cool breeze as I step into the night. 'Fuck prom,' I say as I kick the dirt.

'Now you don't want to be doing that,' a stern voice tells me. I instantly melt. *Angel.*

'No?'

'No,' he says firmly. 'You'll ruin your pretty shoes.' He emerges from the dark shadows of the bushes that frame the doors I just came out of.

'It doesn't matter. I don't think prom is really for me.'

'I thought I might find you out here. You're predictable, you know that?'

'Probably, but I think it's time I go. The reception inside didn't go down so well.'

'No, but that doesn't mean your night has to end. In fact, I think it might just be getting started.' My heart starts to beat faster, and I sneak a look behind me to see if anyone else is taking notice of what is going on out here. They're not.

'Don't be afraid. Come with me.' He's gorgeous. Who wouldn't want to go with him? I eye him cautiously, unaware of his intention. He reaches out for me, his hand waiting for me to put mine in his.

'What if someone sees us?' He smiles, he already knows my fears, but does not share the worry.

'Well, hurry up. No one will see us where we're going.' He curls his fingers, inviting my hand to join with his. I take one last glance around us and try to act brave as I give him what he wants. The second he has my hand he pulls me after him and I struggle to keep up in the heels I'm wearing.

'Where are we going?'

'You'll see.' He leads the way around the back of the building to where the fire exit stairs are. He stops at the bottom of them and looks at me.

'Oh no, you can't be serious?'

'I am, but I promise it will be worth it.' He reaches up and pulls the sliding ladder down until it hits the ground, the metal rattling as it stops against the earth.

'I don't know about this…'

'You're not afraid to be alone with me, are you?' I laugh, because I know he is teasing me.

'Of course not, but I don't really like the thought of climbing up this ladder in heels.'

'Take them off; I'll carry them for you.' The corner of his eyes crinkle, our little adventure already thrilling him and making his features appear younger, like a young boy just learning to ride a bike.

'Okay, but no peeking up my skirt while I scale the tower,' I joke.

'Yes, ma'am.' He salutes and takes my shoes. I giggle as I reach for the first rung and start climbing. The hall is big. Like three stories tall. I climb on, up and up until the ledge of the roof can be felt under my fingertips. He's not too far behind me, I can hear him.

I pull myself up and over, careful not to rip my dress. My eyes are instantly assaulted with the vision before me. So entranced am I, I don't even hear him come up behind me. His fingers graze my bare shoulders, and I jolt from his touch.

'Do you like it?' His voice is whispery, floating from his mouth and then touches my ears gently.

'Why would you do this for me?' I am referring to the decorative state he has transformed the gymnasium rooftop. There are little pink and blue LED lights twinkling around the edges of the brick ledge. It looks magical, and I feel like Rapunzel at the top of her tower. He lets me break free of his touch as I walk to the center of the area he has cordoned off with the lights. It's like our own prom, right here on the roof.

'I hated my prom too, but I still wanted you to enjoy yours. I wanted this to be magical for you.'

'It is,' I whisper as I take it all in. There are flower petals, scattered all over the floor and there is a little table set with a white table cloth and two plastic champagne glasses and a bottle.

'How did you get all this up here? Is that Champagne?'

'Ah it's nothing and, no, that's not Champagne. That would be irresponsible.' I look in his eyes, and we both burst out laughing at the irony. We finish our fit of giggles and calm as we stare deeply into each other's eyes. We can hear the music booming underneath us, the air ducts on the ceiling offering an amplified acoustic as the lyrics float up towards our own private dance floor.

'Would you like to dance, young lady?' One arm hides behind his back as he bows towards me, his other hand extended to ask for a dance.

'Why thank you, kind sir, I accept.' He pulls me into his arms and twirls me around just as *The Miracle of Love* starts to play hauntingly beneath us.

'I love this song,' I say.

'Me too. Eurythmics – they're an oldie but a goodie.' He says no more as he presses his body to mine. We dance slowly, both melting into the wonderful feeling. I rest my head on his shoulder as we sway under the stars. For some reason, they seem more brilliant than I ever remember them being from up here. The pink and blue lights blur into a stream of color as he twirls me around, leading the way in a dance he's done before. I can hear the muffled sound of students in the hall beneath us, but I drown them out and only hear the words of the song.

The miracle of love, will take away your pain.

The words consume me and I feel overcome with emotion. As he holds me tight, a tear slides down my cheek.

'Hey, you're not crying are you?' He pushes me away from him slightly, taking in my appearance.

'No, I'm not,' I lie.

'You are!'

'They're happy tears.'

'Happy tears?'

'Yes. I think this is the nicest thing anyone has ever done for me.'

'Well, I wanted you to have your own private prom, away from people who don't understand you like I do.'

'Thank you. Really, you went to a lot of trouble to set this up and I'm truly grateful.' He pulls me back towards him and wipes the tear from my cheek with his thumb.

'You deserve it. I would do anything for you, you know?' We continue our dance, the lyrics swaying us together. He pulls me close, desperate to comfort me.

I'm being roughly shaken. 'Nooooo,' I cry out. I'm pulled from my glorious memories to pitch blackness, Carron trying to wake me from my beautiful dream.

'No!' I cry out again, sorry that I am so rudely taken out of a memory I cherish so dearly.

'You're dreaming, Bailey. It's okay, honey. You were just having a dream.' His voice is intended to be soothing but I am cross at the intrusion. Damn it! I can't even be with him in my dreams without having him snatched away from me!

'I'm fine,' I say as I roll over and turn my back on him. Carron scoots closer and cuddles me from behind. He is trying to be soothing, but all I want to do is go back to the dream. As I shut my eyes, I pray the dream resumes. There is nothing though, just darkness that fills the void after the beautiful memory.

Four

New York is everything you see on television and more. It's freezing cold in the winter, and yes, there really are that many yellow taxis. The hustle and bustle that weaves through the city leaves chaos and disruption, no chance whatsoever for serenity to blossom while people reside here. There are food vans on every corner block and people selling trinkets and souvenirs to the tourists. All the senses are indulged in this big metropolis, particularly sight, with constant advertising and visuals on every building's façade.

My flight arrives on time so I am delivered to my hotel a couple of hours short of my scheduled meeting. One of the editors from the head office in Boston will be meeting me early afternoon to go over some ideas for the assignment. This leaves me ample time to order a room service lunch and have a hot shower to freshen up. It also means I can quickly send an email.

To: thurmontlumberyard@wizzmail.net
From: bails@quickmail.com
Subject: I need you…
I'm here, are you?
Bails xx

I know there will be no instant reply, so I phone room service and order a chicken and bacon bagel with a side order of fries. While I wait I strip off my clothes and head for the shower.

The water is forceful and hot. It kneads my muscles in the back of my shoulders that have been tense since I left Astoria. There is nervous tension rippling through my body and I am in dire need of some release. But only one person can help me with this, and he's not here to give me what I so desperately need. I hurry and soap my body, taking care to not get my hair wet. It's so long it takes a long while to dry, especially in this weather.

While I'm drying myself I hear a knock at the door. Using the hotel's robe to cover myself I go and open it. A young woman dressed in a hotel uniform places my food on the table for me. I tip her and she leaves me with a smile. My attention does not go straight to the food though. There is the matter of the email I am waiting for and I swipe my finger across my laptop's mouse to wake the screen up. There blinking back at me from my inbox is the gold I'm dying to read.

> *To: bails@quickmail.com*
> *From: thurmontlumberyard@wizzmail.net*
> *Subject: Me*
> *I'll be in later tonight. Dinner?*
> *Angel.*

I quickly hit reply.

To: thurmontlumberyard@wizzmail.net
From: bails@quickmail.com
Subject: Dessert
I'm more preferable to the above.
Bails xx

The scent of my bagel wafts up to me from the plate. My stomach rumbles and I reluctantly dive in while I stare at the computer screen waiting for a reply. It comes moments later.

To: bails@quickmail.com
From: thurmontlumberyard@wizzmail.net
Subject: Patience
You have none. Room number?
Angel.

I'm running out of time and really need to get ready for my meeting. The last of the fries are shoved in my mouth and I quickly tap out my last email to Angel before I see him.

To: thurmontlumberyard@wizzmail.net
From: bails@quickmail.com
Subject: Cannot be helped
807. I need…
Bails xx

There is no reason to tell him what I need. He knows perfectly well, and it would be too dangerous to actually write anything more in an email. Despite the fact that no one reads my emails, I can't be a hundred percent certain it will be the same on his end. I log off and dress in a pair of high-waisted slacks, with heels and a tight-fitting, feminine, crème blouse. I've never been a jeans and T-shirt kind of girl, except for rare occasions. Instead I opt for tailored pants or flowing skirts and dresses. A quick brush through my hair, add some lippy and I'm done.

I'm pretty fortunate with my complexion that I don't need a lot of makeup. I never wear anything on my eyes – they're already so blue and bright that eyeliner or mascara just makes me looks trashy. The fact that I have a smattering of freckles across my nose means I am better off without wearing foundation as it just looks like I am trying to hide something. So I opt for the *au naturel* look. With purse and laptop in arms, I head out of my suite and make my way to the lobby.

Danzar's editor-in-chief, Maria Raftopolous, is the polar opposite of me. We're both twenty-six but she seems to have lived for twice as long as me. Her voice is loud and there are a lot of hand gestures that accompany her when she talks. She has shoulder length thick brown curly hair, a nod towards her Greek heritage. Maria's ass speaks for itself, as do her tits. Whenever we get together I can't help but stare at them, despite my best efforts not to. Her eyebrows are plucked to within an inch of her life and she wears lipstick so bright that her pink lips look like candy.

The Ritz has a private lounge for business meetings and she is waiting for me when I get there. Maria has her trademark skintight mini on and a black flowing blouse that shows her bra through it. She's seated at a corner table that offers views of the city and has a high tea already delivered to the table. I'm pretty full after lunch, but am sure I can fit in one or two of the petite cakes that look enticingly delicious.

'Hey, Maria,' I offer in greeting as I kiss her cheek before sitting across from her.

'Bailey! Wonderful to see you again. Excellent job on the Louis Vuitton spread by the way.'

'Thanks.' She prattles on for a while and I make myself comfortable. This will not be a quick meeting as it is never just about business with Maria. She wants to know everybody's life story because she is the kind of person who would tell a stranger hers. I suspect she finds it particularly difficult to talk to me sometimes because I am a completely closed book. Over the last two years I have been working with her I have come to realize that it is better if I just lie. That way I get her off my back and I've never had to reveal the real me.

By four in the afternoon she finally gets around to giving me a list of content inclusions she wants for the assignment and a list of interview questions she wants answered for the spread. She gives me a business card with an address on it so I can meet the client tomorrow for the interview. They are a new fashion house just opening in the Big Apple and they look set to knock other fashion houses off their pedestals.

While I'm tuning Maria out, I catch a glimpse of the footpath outside and immediately spot Angel walking down the block. Even amongst the sea of people my eyes automatically seek him out. He looks absolutely amazing and my chest explodes into a flutter of heartbeats as I drink him in. He's dressed in jeans and a navy sweater with a white shirt poking out of the top. His hair is still kept short, although the front is a little longer and he has it spiked up. The five o'clock shadow still graces his chiseled jaw and his eyes, even from this distance, have an intensity I just can't ignore. I'm mesmerized and seduced just by looking at him.

'Bailey!' Snapping out of my lusting I turn my attention back to Maria.

'Sorry, what?'

'You weren't even listening to me! Is there some really good piece of ass out there?' She stands slightly to lean towards the window, hoping to afford herself a better view of the people that hurry by on the sidewalk.

'Ah, no. I was just letting my ideas for the assignment run away in my head.' The excuse is poor, but she seems to buy it as she slumps back in her seat.

'And here I was thinking you were actually having fun for a change. Working as usual. You know, Bailey, there really is more to life than just work you know; you should really have some fun while here in New York.'

'You don't say,' I mumble.

'Okay, well it looks like you're good to go tomorrow, give me a call if you need anything, otherwise I'll wait for you to get the article to me by Sunday night.'

We depart ways and I hurry over to the lift. By the looks of things, Angel has just arrived in New York City.

Five

He knows what suite I'm in, I'm just wondering how long it will take before he comes knocking on my door. Or will I have to go to him? The ache inside of me is pulling on every single fiber; it's been far too long since he let me be in his arms. Knowing I can't hold off much longer I decide to call down to reception. The call is answered by a chirpy woman with a nasally voice.

'Hello, this is Bailey Michaels in room 807. I'm just wondering… do you have any messages for me?'

'One moment please, Ms. Michaels.' The phone clicks and the sound of radio music plays over the ear piece. I'm nervous and bite away at my lip while I wait for the receptionist to get back to me.

'Ms. Michaels?'

'Yes?' My breath is held in my chest.

'There's a message for you, to advise you of a room number. The gentleman asked for us to inform you that he'll be staying in room 914.'

'Thank you so much!' I practically squeal as I replace the phone into its receiver. There is no holding me back as I jump on the bed and bounce up and down with excitement. *Okay, just calm down,* I tell myself. The full-length mirror in the entry way of the suite beckons me and I race to give myself a once over. My normally somber expression is lively

51

and bright. My baby blue eyes twinkle back at me with mischief and I'm even showing teeth. That's a smile, in case you couldn't tell. I smooth my long locks into place and quickly apply a smear of cherry lip gloss on my lips. I'm ready.

Taking my room's pass key with me, I close the door and head for the elevator. There is an elderly couple inside who greet me kindly and the old man offers to press the button for the floor I'm after. It's a short ride up to the next floor, and I'm dizzy with the knowledge that Angel is so close.

I thank the couple as I step off onto the ninth floor. The décor is the same as the rest of the hotel except for the art on the walls. There are little brass plaques on the wall indicating which rooms are located where and I follow the directions to room 914. Slowly my eyes seek out each number, dismissing it quickly as I walk on by to find the one I am looking for.

It's only as Angel's room comes into view that my world slowly stops spinning on its axis and grinds to a screeching halt. He's here, I'm here. There is finally breath in my lungs, and it's all because of him. Life in this moment feels complete, so why does he always point out that it is so wrong? I shake the thought from my head. None of that matters right now. Only this moment does.

I knock on the hard wood door and wait. There is a pause before it's flung open and there he stands. My everything is right in this room and all other men cease to exist. *How does he do that?*

'You!' he growls. He stretches out and grabs my arm and drags me into the room. There is nothing on this earth that would have stopped me from following him in there – not even Carron. Not waiting for my brain to catch up, his hands and lips are all over my body the instant he slams the door shut.

My eyes roll into the back of my head as ecstasy takes over. His tall frame presses deeply into mine, locking my body between him and the wall. The five o'clock shadow still covers his face and it grazes my skin as he mauls my neck. I'm panting already and he hasn't even taken my clothes off.

'How could you?' he growls against my body.

'What?' I'm half dazed and not completely capable of coherent conversation right now.

'How could you ask me to come? You know this is so wrong, Bails.' His tongue says otherwise as it trails up to my ear. He sucks hard on the lobe and moves his hands to pull my hair so my head tilts back. I'm eye to eye with the man that holds my heart. His eyes blaze, dark pools of torment that have currents of lust and love swirled deep within. The fleeting moments we share like this are all it takes for me to want to refuse living a normal life if he cannot be in it.

My response chokes in my throat. 'How could I not? I… miss you.' My voice falters, afraid that this may be the last time he ever agrees to see me.

'God, please don't look at me that way! You know I can't refuse you as it is.' His voice catches and it comes out almost like he is begging me. I know he's as tormented as me, but his begging me makes me want him all the more.

'Please, Angel, don't stop. I've waited far too long for your hands to be on me and I can't stand it anymore.' I lick my lips, desperate for his to be on them. His arms snake around my waist and he lifts me up in one fluid movement and carries me to the bed. Gently he places me on the sheets, although the animalistic movements have not left his demeanor. Our history allows me to know that he is just as hungry for this as I am, neither of us feeling guilt or shame now we have come this far. Those emotions only torment us when we are lucid enough to have sense. Insecurity and jealousy have taken a hike too, never festering in the bedroom. It's an innate need to be with each other. It's what made me fall for him the day he saved me. Changed me. Nothing after that day would ever be the same again.

His features are all dark – hair, eyes – even his skin holds a naturally olive complexion. Everything about him draws me in. I watch eagerly as he slowly starts to undress. The lack of shirt reveals a well chiseled chest that could only be achieved from manual labor. He is physically fit from working in the lumber yard and there is nothing I want more than to run my hands all over him. Angel appraises me as I drink him in and the corner of his lips turn up in amusement.

'Do you like what you see?' He's mocking me. He already knows the answer but I nod anyway. The pants are next to go and he's left standing with only his boxer shorts hanging from his hips. Above the waistband the 'V' of his muscles draw my eyes down to his groin. He leaves on his boxers for the moment even though his cock is straining hard against the material. His eyes go back to stalking me and I know his attention has turned back to my own clothes.

'I need you naked… now.' Commanding has always been Angel's way. That's why I love him, depend on him. He's authoritative and used to getting what he wants. But when it comes to me, he knows there are limits.

'Undress me.' The longing inside to feel his firm hands on me is screaming loud and clear. He hears me and takes over my body atop the covers. Gentle but quick, one by one my items of clothing are removed until my pale skin is all that he can see. His lips part, desire taking hold of him and he swiftly takes off what is left of his own clothing.

'Bails, you are so damn breathtaking.' I blush every shade of red as he starts to creep between my legs. His heart-shaped lips trail kisses up my calves, each one teasing a little more out of me. The feeling is so good, I'm in half a mind as to whether I want him to keep teasing me or rush to be inside of me.

Soon he finds his way to the part of me that has been aching for his touch. Kisses turn to licking as he slides his mouth over my clit. I moan, not caring who hears me.

That's all the encouragement he needs. While his mouth goes to work on completely undoing me, his hands are trailing around the tops of my thighs. Pretty soon I can feel his thumb gently rubbing my ass while his tempo increases between my legs. Fisting his hair, I do everything I can to pull him in deeper. My legs wrap around his shoulders and I buck my hips to meet his mouth. I'm close, but I know he won't let me come this way. Angel likes us to come at the same time. He once told me that he feels like we will be connected together forever if our souls clash so wildly while making love. I have never doubted his words.

True to form, he pulls himself from me, leaving me wailing for more even though I know he is about to fulfill me in other ways. His body crushes me as his naked chest meets mine. The feeling of being completely engulfed by him surrenders all my senses. There is nothing that he couldn't ask of me that I would not do. With Angel, anything goes. His lips seek out mine hungrily and I can taste myself on his mouth. The reminder of what he just did arouses me more. While my arms are like twigs next to his, I wrap them possessively around his shoulders and hug him to me.

'I can't stay away from you, Bails.' He moans this over and over between breathless kisses.

'Then don't.' He's heard me beg him a thousand times before. It won't change anything. All we have are these fleeting moments where we can be completely ourselves with each other. My need ensnares him and he starts to push my sex with his cock. He nudges my lips open and forces his way in. I welcome him into my depths with a sigh of contentment. He starts to rock back and forth while I match his rhythm like a shadow. Angel is possessing me, devouring me. In one single act, he completely breaks me down and makes me a slave to his soul.

The frantic pace of our lovemaking increases and I know we are near the end. His head is next to mine and I can hear him breathing erratically into the pillow behind me. I'm struggling for air as his shoulder presses into my windpipe with every thrust he gives me. Emotions are swirling rapidly through me. I'm on the verge of tears as well as ecstasy. There is a precipice I am standing on and I'm a hair's breadth from falling over it.

'Come with me, Bails. I'm ready, baby.' His breath is raspy and his command cannot be ignored. I allow the pleasure to overtake me and as his semen starts to flow inside of me my muscles contract to milk him for all he's worth.

We lay spent and sweaty, entangled in each other. While the beating of my heart slows to a normal pace, a single solitary tear starts to slide down my face.

Six

There is no guilt as my plane makes its descent back into Astoria. All I feel is a loss I have learned to live with. Carron will be picking me up, and my mind is focused heavily on trying to alter my mood. I wonder if he will be able to tell what my body has been through. Will he know that every nerve ending has been set on fire, only to be extinguished before I'm even allowed to let it take hold? All I can do is hope he can't see it.

As is always the case when I have been away on business, the assignment has been a success. But as usual, my heart has been torn out a little more. Tears do no good. Angel is quite adamant that our love affair should never have eventuated in the first place. I try hard to convince him that we are perfect for each other in every way, that he shouldn't let anything come between us. But there will always be that one thing; that one single thing that keeps us apart. I know I will never change his mind, so like the junkie I am I take what I can.

Carron is coming to meet me at the Astoria Regional Airport. By the time the plane lands, I think I have my shit together. In keeping with the way I have always conducted myself around him, I will be neither ecstatic or sad. There is that thin white line that divides the middle of the road and I will happily sit smack bang on it. After the time we have spent together he has come to expect this of me.

The doors to the plane open and I shuffle forward with my carry-on suitcase case like the rest of the passengers. We move like a herd of cattle as we make our way to the baggage claim area. Carron is standing there with a takeaway coffee and a paper under his arm. His glasses are on his face and he looks tired. Even his clothes look rumpled, his jeans seeming like he slept in them too. This week he has been on night shift and the hours show on his face. It is a kind face though, and he affords me a dazzling smile when he sees me. I'm grateful to have him want to spend his life with me. He's a good man – kind and considerate beyond words. His hair is shaggy and unkempt – it is the only physical attribute that does not sing 'doctor' about him.

My eyes find his and I know we will be okay. We will go back to our comfortable lives and the memory of Angel will be pushed back to the darkest parts of my mind until they scream to be thought of again. Carron will never know what lurks there. It is mine and Angel's secret. Only ever ours.

I kiss his cheek and he wraps me in a bear hug.

'Hi there, stranger, I've missed you.' His tone is lighthearted and inviting.

'Hey. I bet you enjoyed yourself while I was gone. Did you get a chance to catch up with Eddy?' Eddy is Carron's closest friend. They usually chill with a couple of beers over a football game, and with his team playing over the weekend I was sure they would have gotten together.

'What? No, "I missed you too"?' He is clearly teasing me. He knows I am never expressive with the mushy stuff between us.

'Of course,' I say, embarrassed. While I know it makes him happy to hear me say this, I feel a tiny stab of guilt – kind of like I am betraying Angel in some way. It's odd, as I'm in a relationship with Carron, but there you go. He kisses the top of my forehead and takes my bag from me.

'Eddy and I had a great time. We ordered pizza in and had a few beers. Of course he was completely pissed his team didn't win.' We walk out of the terminal and towards where Carron has parked his car.

'I'll bet. Too bad for him, but I'm guessing you were thrilled with the results.'

'I'm always happy when my team does well. The Ravens are having a good season, they earned it.' He pops the trunk of the car and puts my bag inside before coming around to open my door for me. I'm about to slide in when he puts his arm across the door to stop me.

'How about a kiss from my favorite girl, huh?' I know it is ridiculous, because I have showered and brushed my teeth several times since I have been with Angel, but there is still a part of my brain that suspects he might be able to smell another man on me. I hold my breath and give him the kind of kiss I reserve for my grandfather. It earns me a weird look from him, but he doesn't say anything. Before he can protest my lackluster mood, I jump into my car seat and buckle up.

'So how was Maria? Did you get your assignment done?' Carron indicates out of the parking garage and heads towards home.

'She's the same old, same old. Well maybe a little louder, I'm not sure. Most of the writing I managed to get completed on the flight back here. The interview went well and I just have to format the text for the page spread James is organizing before I send it off for publication. It should all be straight forward from here.'

I'm comfortable to talk to Carron about my work. It is a safe topic.

'That's great, honey.'

'How about you, been busy at the hospital?'

'Yeah not too bad, although I'll be happy when I go back to the morning shift next week.'

'I still don't know how you do night shift; I'd be a walking zombie.' He chuckles at my description.

'Your mom called while you were away.'

'Oh?' I'm instantly on edge, as I am whenever she calls. It's nothing personal, but every time someone from my home town is in touch I immediately switch to defense mode. I know it has everything to do with Angel and keeping my secret safe.

'What did she say?'

'She said just to call her when you're back. I think she wants to know if we'll be joining your family for Christmas this year.' Carron was a good excuse for getting out of going home last year. I tend to avoid being in my home town at all costs, because I know I would just die if I saw *him* there. As far as odds go, there is every possibility that Angel will also go home for Christmas. It's enough of an emotional drain to run into any of the girls who were there that day. Chevy Chase is the kind of town where everyone knows everyone. I know they still remember who I am, despite my eight year absence.

'I'll call her later.'

'We should really go to your folks this year, Bails.' He takes his attention off the road for a second to appraise me.

'I know.'

'It will be fun. I haven't been back to Washington DC in a long time – we could go see the White House while we're there.' He's trying to be enthusiastic for my sake, but I'm struggling to share his enthusiasm.

'Yay!' My tone is dripping with sarcasm.

'Don't be a spoil sport. Your parents and your brother are dying to see you, you know.' And there's the deal breaker right there.

'Okay,' I huff. 'I'll call her tonight.'

'That's my girl.' He grins like a Cheshire cat as he swings the car onto our street.

***

The talk with my mother is going better than I expected. When I tell her Carron and I will be coming home for Christmas she is ecstatic, yelling to my father in the background about the good news. I'm actually really pleased I will be seeing my family, it's just the memory of my home town that runs like a cold knife down my back. There is nothing that can hurt me there anymore, but sometimes the fear is actually worse than the reality. Being brave has never really been my thing. I guess that is why I needed Angel to save me in the first place, and why I now rely on Carron to bring some sort of normalcy to my day to day life.

Mom doesn't make mention of my brother being home for Christmas, so I leave her to prattle on for a minute. My brother came into our lives when I was just two. His birth mother was a drug addict who let her pimp sell her body on the streets for anything he could to earn a dime to buy drugs with. State services finally took him from her when he was just five years old and sent him to live in our foster care. His mother never got him back because she died from an overdose. With no legal guardian to show up for the court hearing, our family was appointed his custodians until he turned eighteen. The whole family was thrilled to bits. Mom and Dad got the son they'd always wanted and I got a brother to play with.

We end our telephone call with my mom on a good note. She's tickled pink, the excitement in her voice bubbling over. I'm happy we will all get to see each other over the festive season and tell her so.

'Aww, me too, honey. You tell Carron we're looking forward to seeing him now won't you dear.'

'Sure, Mom, I'll tell him.'

'Okay, sweetie. Your dad sends his love and we'll see you in a few weeks okay?'

'No worries, give Dad my love too.' We hang up and Carron is staring at me from across the bench top. The bemused smile on his face makes him look endearing and he kind of reminds me of my dad in a way.

'What?'

'That wasn't so hard now, was it?'

'No. I'm just not a fan of Chevy Chase.'

'The actor or the place?' I poke my tongue out at him and throw the tea towel that is sitting on the kitchen bench at him.

'The place of course.'

'I don't know why that is, you've never told me you know.' His eyebrows are raised in question, but it is not one I will ever answer. Some things are just best left unsaid.

'And I never will.' His large smooth hands come up in protest.

'Fine, fine. But you can trust me you know? I mean, if you ever want to talk about it.' His smile is kind, but my heart stays firmly shut.

'I'm all good, but thanks. I'm just gonna go have a shower before dinner if you're okay to finish off preparing by yourself.'

'Go ahead, I'm just about done here anyway.' I stop in my tracks. Fuck. I'm such a shit and I know it. This man loves me to pieces and I just take him for granted. It's not something I can help doing – but he lets me. Repeatedly. His carefree attitude is what brings me some kind of solace in my day to day life, and yet I offer him nothing personal about myself in return. I know I am too ruined to really be in a relationship with anyone, but I can't help clinging on to the fact that he brings me comfort. Comfort when I am missing Angel to death. I shake my head. Thoughts of Angel should not be occupying my mind while I am here with Carron.

I walk over to Carron and put my hands around his waist and snuggle into his chest. 'Thank you,' I say, muffled against his sweater. His body tenses for a second before completely relaxing again. He rubs my arms that are wrapped around him tightly.

'For what, Bails?'

'For just being you.' With a final squeeze I take my departure for the shower before he has time to delve into that line of conversation anymore. By the time my foot hits the first of the stairs I know his eyes are on me. I can feel them burning on my back, through my clothing like hot coals. He stares after me because he is trying to figure me out. This I know, because I have seen the look many times before. But I know that he will never figure me out. For him to do that, he would have to really know me. Instead, I let him live with the lie.

Seven

Morning brings the kind of day that makes me want to stay in bed. Jezebel is snuggled on the end of the covers at my feet, which warms me somewhat. Even with her heating my toes and Carron's body next to mine, I can still feel the chill in the air. I roll over onto my side and stare at him while he sleeps. His hair is tousled and the hair on his face has grown so much in the last week it is starting to look like a proper beard. He's very handsome. Dependable. He is my security blanket as I navigate through life. I am honest enough to admit that I depend on him being around. Sometimes I wish I could be in his head just for a minute to know what he really thinks of me.

The urge to pee becomes unbearable and I slip out of the covers and make my way to the bathroom. While I'm there I quickly brush my teeth before heading back to bed. As I slip between the sheets, Carron stirs next to me.

'Good morning, beautiful.' His voice is husky from not being used overnight. He has not yet opened his eyes, but his hand reaches out to find my body among the covers. With a firm tug of the waistband of my pyjama bottoms, I slide easily into his arms.

'Morning, sorry I woke you.'

'I'm glad you did.' He nudges his erection against my thigh. There is nothing Carron likes more than morning sex.

A creature of habit, I have come to expect that this is our routine. Evenings we are both normally too shattered to share any intimacy and usually are both asleep before our heads even hit the pillow.

There is none of the urgency I feel when I am with Angel. Carron is all about the tenderness. I let him take the lead as he awakens from his slumber. His hands roam gently over my body – a soft squeeze here, a little touch there. My lips find his and we kiss gently, my minty breath mixing with his. Palms find my breasts and he cups them easily, rubbing softly over my nipples. My body responds to his touch and I feel arousal deep in the pit of my belly.

'Make love to me,' I urge him.

'Oh, I intend to.'

Slowly he strips my garments off. I am chilled by the air every time he ruffles the covers. The cat decides she is not wanted here and scurries out the room.

'About time that damn cat took off.'

'Leave her,' I scold, and he turns his attention back to my body.

As usual he is naked and it takes him no time at all to get me undressed. He rolls on top of me and the heat from his skin warms me somewhat. Staring into his eyes I can see my auburn hair swirling around in there. Carron is fully awake now and staring at me intently. His mouth dips to take mine and at the same time his cock snakes its way up between my legs. They part willingly because I know that he is going to satisfy me very soon.

With a gentle push he is inside of me and he groans as his cock sinks deeper inside of me. I wrap my legs around his and leverage his body in and out of mine. This goes on for a while. Carron isn't urgent or brash, he takes his time. We rock back and forth, the aching deep inside of me being gently stroked until I want to come. I start to breathe heavier as I let my body go, and it is a bittersweet moment when I do. Betrayal sweeps over me rapidly and it is all I can do not to shove him off me and run from the room. Repeatedly I scream at myself to stop doing this to myself – to him. Breathing rapidly I struggle to compose myself as he brings himself to orgasm. His cock penetrates me as he pulses and shudders inside of me.

We lay still, both in our own worlds. Finally he pulls out and moves clumsily to get off me.

'Come and join me for a shower?'

'Mmm.' It's all I can say right now. Carron takes off for the bathroom as I slowly rise to follow him.

'How about we grab coffee and take a walk up to The Column today?' His voice echoes around the tiles in the bathroom as he talks.

'Sounds good,' I call after him. Someday soon I'm sure he's going to kick my miserable ass to the curb. In the meantime, I'm going to avoid the truth and take advantage of his kindness, keeping him here as long as he will stay.

Eight

With Carron and I only getting limited time off over Christmas, we decide to fly to Washington DC and get a hire car from there. We arrive at Washington Dulles International Airport at ten in the morning, two days before Christmas. The airport is packed with vacation travelers and we fight through the sea of people to get to the car hire station. We wait more than half an hour for our turn with the cashier, and I'm thankful Carron had the good sense to book ahead.

Once all the paperwork is sorted and we have they keys, we head out the exit doors in search of our vehicle. Out of the airport terminal, traffic is just as heavy as it had been in the parking lot. My home town isn't far from the airport, but with traffic the way it is today it takes us twenty-three minutes just to get to the edges of Chevy Chase.

My family house is located in Northampton Street NW in Upper Chevy Chase. We drive past St John's College High School, where I went as a teenager. There are some bad memories there, some good. I try not to dwell on either, but already I'm looking for Angel. I wonder if he is home for Christmas, or whether work is too busy to get here. To be honest I don't know what I would do if I did see him, especially if I am with Carron at the time.

As though the universe is playing some cruel joke on me, I see him from the car window. My heart races at the sight of him and I instantly want to call out to him. Carron observes none of my behavior – his eyes are glued to the road and he is navigating in a town he's only been to once before. My amazed gawking continues as our car rolls past him. He's in sweats, out jogging in the frigid air. Despite the fact he has a hoodie on, I know it is him. His jaw line juts out just so and his dark hair spikes out from the top of the hood. Angel has the grace of an athlete when he runs. I should know, I've seen him using the school oval on many occasions. I'm entranced by the fog streaming from his mouth as his lungs exert to pump air through them. All too quickly he is gone, and I am left to wonder if it was just a dream.

So, he had come back to town after all. Did he know I'd be here? I'm startled out of my haze when I realize Carron is talking to me.

'Sorry, what?'

'Earth to Bailey, I wanted to know if you'd mind if I stopped by the liquor store before we go to your folks' place?'

'No, I don't mind,' I murmur.

'Great, because I want to get your dad a really nice bottle of scotch and some red wine to go with dinner.'

'Don't tell me you're already thinking about dinner!' Carron has to be the only male foodie I know; he lives to eat instead of eating to live. He's lucky his genes allow him to do this without wearing all that food.

'Hey, no judging all right, you know your mom is the best cook I know.'

'I'm not judging, I'm just in awe of your eating capabilities. You know you just ate lunch right?' I am referring to the sandwich and blueberry muffin he scoffed on the plane.

'That was a snack!'

'A snack?' I scoff. 'You had better not complain this year that you're too full to do anything or I'm going to go out without you, you know.'

'Yeah, yeah, I hear ya.' His tone is light and jovial. He's happy to be having some time off from work. He pulls into the local liquor store and we both get out of the car. I know it's crazy, but as I follow Carron inside I find myself scanning the footpath, half expecting Angel to just come on trotting by. I leave Carron to do the shopping and just trail behind while he makes his purchases. When he's made his selection, we head back to the car and make the last couple of turns until we end up on my parents' street.

Their home is beautiful. I loved living here as a child and have to admit I still enjoy coming back and spending time in my old room. My mom never changed it; she left it just the way I did when I moved out. There is the American flag flying ceremoniously out the front of a two-storey white clapboard house. The trees surrounding it have grown lush and green over the years and it lends itself to the surrounding beauty of the neighborhood. I love the big bay window that extends from the side of the house. When I was a little girl I used to sit on the boxed window seat with a hot chocolate during the winter months and stare for hours as the snowflakes dropped outside. The leaves are a little bare now, but I know it will return to its finery once spring arrives again.

Carron swings the car into the driveway and applies the handbrake.

'Ready?' he asks, but there is no time for a reply. My mother has been watching that front window like a hawk for that last hour or so, awaiting our arrival with anticipation. Even through the glass of the car windows I can hear her clearly shouting to my dad.

'They're here, George, quick come along now!' I smile at her exuberance. She has always been the kind of person to openly display her emotions – even to strangers. 'Wears her heart on her sleeve,' my dad always said. I take after him. He feels a lot, but you would be hard pressed to see it on his face. Unless you know him really well of course. Which I do.

Mom rushes the car and pulls my door open for me and I am met by a gust of cold air.

'Hey, Mom.'

'Oh darling, it's so good to see you!' She pulls me out of the car and wraps her arms around me. I cuddle her warmly and take in her scent. It's so comforting to be in her arms that I instantly relax. She smells like Jasmine and Pears soap. There is a little more meat on her bones than when I saw her last, but she is still my mom and that will never change.

'I've missed you.' My voice catches in the back of my throat and I feel like the worst daughter ever. I should come home more often; I know I don't get back nearly as much as my parents would like.

'I've missed you too, sweetheart. Now come on in out of the cold and say hello to your dad and brother.' She turns her attention to Carron then and scoots around to his side of the car to embrace him as her future son-in-law. Sometimes the word *fiancé* still gets stuck in the back of my throat. I grab my bag off the back seat and head up the foot path, Carron and Mom's chatter lively behind me.

The minute I step in the front door my dad comes to greet me. We have always been close and I miss the time we spent together while I was growing up. I'm similar to him in many ways. We share the same personality for starters, but also the same physical attributes: tall, lanky and good bone structure. His hair is a little redder than mine, but I am definitely this man's daughter.

'Hey, Bails, how's my favorite daughter doing?' He squeezes me tight and I take the chance to inhale his aftershave. It is my most favorite smell in the world. The scent alone evokes so many memories that I get lost in a trip down memory lane just hugging him.

'Dad, I'm your only daughter, remember?'

'Of course I remember, that's why you're my favorite.' I laugh as he jokes with me and we move past the foyer. In front of me is the wide flight of stairs that goes up to the bedrooms. I hear the creak of them before I see the person.

'Ah, here's your brother too. I finally get the chance to have both of my kids home for vacation.' My dad is beyond happy right now. In fact, I haven't seen him this excited since he met Ronald Reagan (the man responsible for Reagan being my middle name).

'Hi guys.' He takes the stairs two at a time until he is in front of us. He kisses my cheek lightly before offering his hand to Carron.

'Hey, Emmett, how're you doing?' Carron is the epitome of the perfect guest. He's polite beyond belief and has impeccable manners. He's the kind of person you never have to worry about introducing to anyone.

'Well, thanks, and you?' My brother is short, clipped even. He doesn't really care how Carron is in the slightest. He doesn't like Carron, but hey, I am not allowed to tell him who he can and cannot like. Ever since I brought him home a year and a half ago to meet my parents Carron's been on Emmett's shit list.

My mother is aware of the vibe that is passing between the two and hurries to dissolve any friction in the air.

'Carron, can I offer you a drink?'

'That would be great, Kathy,' he replies as we are huddled off into the den.

And so the fun begins.

Nine

By nightfall we are all inebriated enough not to give a rat's ass whose company we are in. My mother has been baking up a storm and drinking the liquor meant for cooking as she goes along. She's merry beyond belief and is in her own little world as she trots about the house, filling people's glasses and offering them more food. The rum balls are her specialty and I spy Carron scoffing more than his fair share. We play gin rummy while we finish off the red wine that we came with.

'I'm off to bed,' says Emmett. He's a sore loser – always has been.

'Goodnight, Son.' My dad smiles mischievously. I think he may be cheating again. The rest of us play a little longer before taking ourselves up to bed. Carron and I retreat to my bedroom, and I have to laugh at the fact my parents have left two single beds in here.

'What are you giggling at?' Carron is playful; he's never been a bad drunk.

'The beds.'

'Surely your mom doesn't think a single bed is going to keep me from getting into your panties.' He grins salaciously at me and starts to waggle his eyebrows.

'It damn well better!' I hiss. 'That bed there squeaks and there is no way I am having sex in my parents' house when there are three other sets of ears to hear us.'

'You're no fun,' he grumbles and he reaches into his toiletries bag for his toothbrush.

'You'll thank me later,' I call after him as he heads for the bathroom and I hear him faintly down the hall saying, 'I don't think so.' I hurry to change into my pyjamas and grab my toothbrush also. Carron and I pass each other in the hall and I can see by the droopiness of his eyelids that he will be asleep before I even make it back into the room.

I'm proven right five minutes later. He's snoring loudly when I come back into the bedroom. Gently, I roll him onto his side and he shuts up instantly. When I slide into the sheets, I remember what it was like to live here as a teenager and my thoughts turn to Angel.

There is something so primal about needing him that I almost wail. If I wasn't so inebriated and docile right now I would leave Carron to his dreams and run to Angel. My mind tracks back to that day. I had always been such an ugly duckling. Really, I mean it. I was all gangly limbs and braces. But I never saw myself as the geek, rather that title was assumed for me by others at my high school. If I had any sense I would have seen the attack coming long before it happened.

One day there was a note on my locker. It read *Come down to the old Oak Willow in fifth period.* The school borders a nature reserve, but everyone knew the tree simply because its girth was so wide. Ever the curious I went there. I don't even know why I did. I didn't really have any friends outside of my book club and they would have just come and talked to me – not asked me to meet them somewhere.

But I went, the note seemingly clandestine and mysterious. It was a warm afternoon and I had on a yellow sun dress. I remember it vividly because I had to throw it out after that day and it was my favorite at the time. When I got to the tree I waited for ten minutes before Alva Trilby and her posse of friends showed up. I knew who Alva was, I mean in high school *everybody* knows who the most popular kid is. What shocked me was that she had asked me to come and meet her. The minute I saw her I just thought *why?*

After several minutes of enduring her screaming at me it dawned on me what she was saying. She'd overheard her footballer boyfriend talking to some friends. He had expressed that I 'had a fine ass' and she was pissed about it. To be honest I wasn't really that worried about the whole thing because I was ready to laugh it off. That was until her tone took on a hysterical pitch and fear started to creep its way into my bones. When her body language became threatening I started to wonder if I should just make a run for it. That's when she screamed, 'It's time we teach this little bitch a lesson.' Before I knew it, I had three seniors all throwing themselves at me. They were irate and I could feel the force of their venom in each and every blow. After five minutes I wished I could just die.

My left eye started to close up and I was on the grass with a swollen lip. I was sure one of them had cracked a rib when her foot had landed there. I instantly felt like vomiting. Not one of them was showing me any mercy and I began to wonder if they would ever let up. All I could do was throw my arms up around my head to try and protect myself from their angry outburst. It was while I was on the ground that I saw him. It was out of my good eye that peeked between my fingers that he came into my vision.

Dark, furious, handsome. He literally came flying at us with such speed he knocked Alva and her co-conspirators well away from my body. The relief at him coming to my rescue had me racking with sobs. He didn't pick me up straight away. He later told me he was so filled with rage he only saw the others. Girls or not, there was no kindness in his treatment towards them. He kicked the living shit out of each and every one of them, and threatened if they ever told a soul he would come back and do it all over again.

Some of them ended up in hospital that day, but I was the only one who ended up in the arms of her savior. Not one of us ever told anyone the truth about what happened. Eventually Alva moved away, as did the other two. Even I moved as soon as I was able. But not because of the incident, despite how traumatic it was.

I moved away because I found myself in love with Angel. If there was one person in school who was completely off limits, it was him.

Ten

I know that if I want to see him alone, I am going to have to do it on his terms. Morning brings with it frost and a nasty chill in the air. Carron is snuggled deep under the covers and snoring softly. Slowly I slide from under his grasp before quickly shrugging on a tracksuit and jacket. Normally I am no exercise queen, but this morning I am going to damn well pretend I am.

Downstairs my dad is already having his morning coffee. It is his ritual to read the paper while downing French toast and drinking coffee. I kiss the top of his head and I make my way to the back door. His eyes trail after me, watching over the top of his specs.

'Where are you off to at this hour?'

'I'm just going to take Frankie for a walk. I promised him last time I was here.' He doesn't look convinced, and looks to his pug dog as though he would have some answers.

'Really, at this hour? I didn't have you pegged for the sporty type, sweetie.' He's mocking me and I know it. My dad and brother were always the athletic ones in the family, with mom and I always being the butt of their jokes while growing up.

'Yes, Dad,' I huff.

'Okay, well if you're sure, honey, just be careful – there's a lot of ice out there today.'

'You bet.' With a soft whistle, Frankie leaves his bed near the stove and comes to meet me at the back door.

'You want to go walkies, Frankie?' He whines, but I take that as a yes. Outside is bordering on freezing, but there is nothing that will stop me from heading out. I'm off to go to the last place on earth I want to be – my old high school.

The fear should keep me away, but I know it is the one place that he could possibly be alone. I know this because it is a meeting place of sorts. Whenever I am back in town at the same time as him, he always finds me there. Perhaps this is because it's the one place where everything in our lives changed.

Crunching through the frost I hurry with the dog down the streets. Traffic on the road is light and many people are still in bed. The trees are listless with no leaves or wind moving them to show they are alive. The school is not far, but already I can feel the anticipation creeping over me. By the time I reach the school grounds, I'm nervous as hell. I know he is already here, I can feel he's close.

Heading towards the rear of the school, I know I will find him on the oval. I'm not disappointed when I see a familiar figure running laps, powerful and impressive in his movements. Angel is like a well-oiled machine, arms and legs moving in perfect synchronization as his body works hard to beat out a steady rhythm.

Frankie whines. 'Oh don't be such a big baby, no one will see us.' I know my reassurances are more for myself than him. Taking the concrete stairs two at a time I make my way to the lower half of the oval where the track and field events are always held. It's hard for me to even put one foot in front of the other. Not just because this was where I was attacked, but because right now, *he* is here. Like the planets are aligning, he turns from where he is on the other side of the field and takes in the company that has just joined him.

He immediately changes course and sprints for all he's worth in my direction. While he doesn't look as furious as he did that day, I can clearly see the animal within. Definitely with all the grace of a panther, his looks match the beast too. The blur of darkness rushes towards me without any hesitation. As he nears me, I am able to focus on him more clearly and see that most of the dark coloring is his sweat suit covering his muscular frame. His hood is in place on his head just like when I saw him jogging the other day. The dark tufts of his hair are sticking out from underneath the rim of it. I stand perfectly still, waiting for him.

When he just about reaches me he pulls up short and tentatively takes the last few steps in a painfully slow gait. He's stalking me, eyes roaming over the planes of my body that I wish his hands were touching instead. Five inches from my lips he stops and breathes heavily.

Despite the cold, he's sweating. His face is flushed from his exertion and it makes me turn a brighter shade of pink to remember this is how his face usually looks when we make love – when we become one. He can see the desire in my eyes; it is reflected in his also. Frankie sits patiently on the frost bitten grass, waiting until I am ready to continue our walk again.

Angel inches closer and starts to circle me. When he comes to stand directly behind me he stops and leans in, so that when he speaks I can feel his breath on the back of my neck and it makes the hairs on my arms stand on end.

'What the fuck are you doing back in town?' he growls. My breath catches sharply in the back of my throat at the tone of his voice. It is dark and husky, demanding and forceful.

'I… ah, was hoping I would see you.' It's lame, but the truth.

'You know you should have told me you were coming! How the fuck am I supposed to move around town when you're here?' He leans in closer and pulls on my arms so that my back falls against his chest. The warmth of his body lulls me into his spell and I am putty in his hands. He could ask anything of me at this moment and I would have to say yes. Except if it was one of his ridiculous demands that I never see him again – that is one thing I will never agree to. His lips find my neck and he starts kissing me, his breath hot and feverish against my skin.

Immediately I respond between my legs. The ache for him is suddenly turned up to full wattage and I need to be stroked by him.

'How can I think of anything else when you are so close to me?' He is anxious, needing answers I just don't have.

'I don't know,' I sigh, and let my head fall back against his shoulder. The dog still sits while I am swept up into Angel's world.

'Please… touch me,' I beg.

'This is so wrong; you know I shouldn't have laid a finger on you to start with. There are always so many consequences, even now.' His voice is rough but filled with so much desire it can't be ignored.

'I don't care about what's right or wrong, all I care about is you. You and me. Do you remember that day?'

'Of course I do,' he says between kissing my neck.

'I think about it all the time. If you hadn't come to save me I don't know what would have happened.'

'There was no way I was going to let those girls hurt you.' His voice has taken on a serious tone and I don't want to get him angry by making him remember something he would rather forget.

'I know, but I fell in love with you that day. As wrong as that may be, I still want it, I still need it. I need you.' As usual I want to cry. There is nothing on this earth I want more than him, but he will never give himself to me. He would never allow our relationship to become acceptable to him. And yet, we still have these run-ins, where our souls collide for just a moment in time before he makes me leave.

'You know I love you, right?' he sighs into my neck.

'Yes,' I whisper.

'So please just accept that this is the way we have to be.' As loud as I can in my head I scream. *NEVER! Never, never, never!* I will never give up on him, despite the fact he keeps insisting I move on with my life. Move on with Carron.

'Please touch me,' I beg of him.

'Why?'

'Because I can't stand you not to, especially when you are so close.'

'Bailey...' It's a warning that I will not heed.

'Please, Angel, please touch me!' He does, and it is wonderful. It is all I can do not to cry out with happiness. His hot mouth is on my neck and his arms snake around to the front of my body. I can feel his erection pressed up against my backside and I grind myself against him, wanting to touch any bit of him I can. My hands reach past my sides and grab onto his thighs. They are strong and muscled from all the running he does. I squeeze firmly, needing in my own way to possess him.

One of his hands cups my breast while the other worms its way into the front of my tracksuit pants. My breath sucks in as his fingers roughly shove my panties to the side and he starts to explore the folds of my pussy. He finds my clit and starts to stroke me softly. It is all I can do not to rub myself harder against his fingers as he brings my body towards release.

'More, please more.' I'm panting and sound a lot like Frankie does when I take him for a walk. Only I am sure I'm getting more pleasure out of this than the dog does his outings. Angel slides two fingers deep inside of me while his thumb continues to rub my clit. Here out in the open, smack bang in the middle of the high school field, I am in heaven. Thankfully the whole school is on Christmas vacation which has left the place deserted for our enjoyment.

'Do you like that?' He asks me, although I am barely capable of words right now.

'Yes, oh yes. Please don't stop, Angel.'

'Say my name again.'

'Angel. Angel, Angel, Angel.' His grip on me tightens and his fingers swirl around inside my depths, moving at a much faster pace than what he was just a moment ago. My legs begin to feel like jelly and I am barely capable of standing.

'I'm gonna come,' I wail.

'Yes, baby, come.' And I do. My body shatters around his fingers, my orgasm rocking me all the way to the ground. I feel the muscles inside my pussy clench over and over as the spasms take control of me. Finally, when I am still, he slowly slides his fingers out of me. I turn to see his lustful eyes burning into me. He licks his fingers in front of me, sucking the juices from my pussy that covers them.

'That is so gross,' I say, shaking my head at him.

'Damn you taste good.' He is grinning like a kid – like the more youthful man I fell in love with eleven years ago. Angel hasn't changed a bit.

'I have to go.' Dark clouds seem to hang over him as he says this.

'Don't.'

'You know I have to.'

'I don't want you to, please, just stay with me for once.'

'You know that's not possible.' He kisses me briefly and I can taste the lingering metallic juices of my pussy on his lips. His tenderness zaps me out of my senses and I am still standing there with my eyes closed while he is already turning to make his leave. Blinking to refocus, I drink in his solid frame as he walks away from me.

'Ever?' I yell after him as loud as I can. He stops dead. I'm actually dumbstruck. For him to stop is a little victory in itself. *Never say never,* I sing to myself. He turns to face me.

I wither under his gaze. It is intense. He contemplates a minute and then gives me a full blown grin before taking off across the field at a sprint.

Right about now I feel a little victorious. At least that wasn't a no.

Eleven

In a bit of a daze, I walk back towards home with Frankie. He seems very pleased with himself, as do I. We arrive back at the house, and the minute we enter the kitchen I see that my mom is up and bustling about making bacon and pancakes for everyone.

'Morning, Mom.' I kiss her cheek as she pours my dad more coffee.

'Good morning, dear. Goodness gracious your cheeks are cold. Would you like coffee?'

'I might make tea thanks. Is Carron up?' I'm praying he hasn't gotten out of bed yet and noticed my absence.

'Not yet, dear, although breakfast will be ready shortly. Why don't you go wake him?'

'Okay, I'll be back in just a minute.' Trepidation fills me as I climb the stairs and make my way to my old bedroom. Carrying around a guilty conscience sucks big balls. Already I am thinking that he will be able to smell Angel on me, catch a trace of his scent lingering about my body parts. Perhaps taste something amiss on my lips if he wants to kiss me. I know I am completely deceitful and taking complete advantage of Carron. Knowing this makes me think that perhaps I want him to find out about the affair. At least then everything would be out in the open and I could stop lying to myself. And everyone else for that matter.

Sensibility reigns in hard before I reach my room. I quickly duck into the bathroom to brush my teeth and wash my face and neck, trying to rid myself of another man's smell. Carron is still twisted in the sheets, although he stirs when I enter the room and the door creaks.

'Hey,' he mumbles sleepily.

'Hey yourself. Get up, lazy bones, you're sleeping the day away.'

'What time is it?'

'It's already 9:15 a.m. and Mom's got breakfast ready downstairs with a fresh jug of brewed coffee. You'd best hurry before we clear up and start getting Christmas dinner prepared for tomorrow.' I yank the sheets off for effect and reveal his naked body in the process.

'Fuck, Bails, it's goddamn freezing!'

'That'll teach you to wear clothes,' I snicker. I'm not sure if he is appreciating all my sass, but he quickly grabs his clothes and chases after me. He catches me on the landing and envelopes me with his long arms. There is nothing I can do when he twists me to face him and he plants a huge kiss on my lips.

'Mmm, you smell like soap and toothpaste,' he says, sniffing me. You can bet your ass I am damn thankful I just washed and brushed.

'Yeah, it's called hygiene, of which you could use some by the way.'

'Hey, no fair! My morning breath isn't that bad!'

'Says who?' For some reason I am loving tormenting him today. Playful me – this is something new.

'Says me. Now lead the way missy, this man has a bear sized appetite and I'm going to need lots of food to get me through this cold winter.' Carron lowers his voice to mimic that of a bear too. It's actually kinda cute.

'Okay, but keep your paws to yourself, my parents are up you know.'

'Oh I forgot, they've never seen a couple show affection for each other before!' I spin around and take a swipe at him.

'Smart ass,' I hiss. He smiles a great big goofy grin and his hazel eyes are twinkling with satisfaction.

'Lead the way, ma'am.' I give him my best stink eye and then lead him to the kitchen where Mom is serving up loads of crispy bacon and piping hot pancakes.

'Good morning, Carron. Coffee?' My mom has this inbuilt need to serve people. I'm sure she was a slave in a past life. She doesn't wait for a reply, because to her the question is a moot point. He's getting coffee whether he wants it or not. We hungrily tear into the food before us and sit back with a contented sigh when our plates are clean.

'Gee, Mrs. Michaels, I don't know how Bailey stayed so slim with all your amazing cooking while she was growing up.'

'Good genes, dear!' she responds. My dad scoffs.

'Well Bailey wasn't always the best of eaters you know. When she was thirteen she refused to eat anything that wasn't pink. What a hoot that was! We hassled her like nobody's business, trying to get her to eat her meals. She was such a stubborn little thing.' He says this proudly. Carron is grinning big time, looking at me like he is just discovering a whole new side of me.

'So how'd you get her to eat her food then?'

'Stop it, Carron, you don't need to know. You're all embarrassing me!'

'Don't be silly, dear, Carron's practically family. Tell him, George,' says Mom with a smile. Traitor.

'Well Emmett came up with a genius plan to use red food dye. He put it in everything. Pink pancakes, pink cauliflower, pink bread – you name it. If it was white, Emmett was in the kitchen dying it a different color!'

'Really? That's so funny! I can't believe you were such a fussy pants,' he says pointedly, looking at me with renewed interest. 'So how long did that go on for?'

'Months,' says Dad, 'but she got sick of it eventually and moved onto some other fad that took her fancy.' They're all laughing now, quite enjoying my past eating habits. I get up to leave the table, but Mom interjects before I scuttle off with cheeks as pink as the food I once liked.

'Now I've sent Emmett to pick up the alcohol for tomorrow and I was just wondering if you and Carron would mind to go to the shops for the few bits I missed from my shopping list?'

'Sure, Mom.'

'Great, dear, I'll just grab it for you.' We clear the plates and grab the list from my mom with strict instructions from her on where to go to get the produce she's after. Carron and I head out for what I think is going to be a simple trip to the shops.

***

My life is never simple. I'm still stupid enough to think this town is big enough for the both of us. We no sooner hit the indoor vegetable markets and who should I spy across the vast interior but Angel. It is impossible not to notice him. His dark looks draw me in every time. One minute there is a mass of people, and the next all I see is him. His arms are full of gift-wrapped presents. He notices me too and I can see him frowning. Stupidly I wonder what is up his ass after our intense encounter this morning, until I realize it is all to do with the company I am keeping. Carron, as usual, is oblivious to all that is going on around him.

'Carron?'

'Yeah?' He's busy looking at the list of ingredients we need.

'Can you do without me for a minute? I just need to go to the bathroom.'

'Sure, babe, I'll still be here when you get back.' He smiles and then goes back to what he was doing. Hard not to like him, believe me I know.

I take my time and wander off in search of the nearest toilets which are located right in the corner of the building down a darkened corridor. A lady comes out of the stall and holds it open for me. It is a single cubicle set up, although there is one for males next door. I'm just about to lock it when I feel the door pulled out of my grasp. On the other side is Angel. Despite the fact I knew he would follow me here, I still gasp when I see him. He shuts the door immediately and turns his blazing glare upon me.

'Just tell me one thing, Bails, why the fuck did you bring him here with you?'

'I… ah…'

'I mean, is it just to torture me? Because it's working you know!' I'm snapped out of my fumbling by his words. They cut me to the core.

'What the hell are you talking about? I'm with Carron because you insisted on it in first place! You said to me I could never be with you. You said that I should move on and be with someone else. You practically forced me to be with him because *you* refuse to be with me! The last time you cut off contact it almost killed me!' A sob catches in the back of my throat and I am close to tears. I start to tremble with anger. I hate feeling like this: like I am always doing something wrong and hurting people. Angel knows he has upset me, but I'm beginning to think maybe it's time I moved on from him once and for all.

He grabs me around the waist and crushes his lips to mine, pulling me so tightly to him that I can't breathe. His tongue finds mine and I instantly succumb to his spell.

'I can't stand it any longer, Bails. I want you all to myself,' he growls.

And then he goes and says that.

Twelve

With our vacation out of the way, we board the plane to head back to Astoria. Carron has work to get back to and I know I'm going to have assignments waiting for me on my email account. I am willing to bet there will also be an email from Angel there too. I'm still running circles in my head, trying to make sense of every conversation we have ever had. Trying to place where I may have misinterpreted what was spoken between us. There is nothing that stands out, but then again it may just have been my misunderstanding.

How can he say one minute he wants me to move on from him and then make love to me the next? Why would he say that I should start dating other people, and then look like he wants to murder his replacement every time he lays eyes on him? What would possess him to refuse to see me, only to have him email me in the next breath saying he simply must see me! The whole thing is starting to mess with my head and I'm mentally exhausted from trying to figure him out.

Angel has always been complicated, even when I was in school. He didn't talk to many people and many of the kids avoided him. *Intense* was a word that seemed to follow him around. Even I didn't have much to do with him at school before he came to my rescue. I was always the library girl, a member of the math club and the school newspaper's editor.

He liked rock music and tended to drink at school on a Friday afternoon before classes even broke up. I know this because I overheard him and the principle having heated words with each other one day.

Carron and I are seated in the airplane flying somewhere over Washington DC. He has those idiotic eye masks on that are supposed to help you sleep. I reckon they just lull you into a false sense of security so that you are stupid enough to relax and drool over the person next to you. Lucky me. The flight attendant offers me a beverage but I decline, thinking that this would be a good time for me to get some shut-eye too.

I recline my chair as far as it will go and wrap my cardigan around me tightly. There was a little luck on my side when I snared the window seat. With my pillow propped against the wall, I rest my head against it and close my eyes. It's not long before I'm dreaming and as usual my head is filled with thoughts of Angel.

An older me is watching the scene, kind of like an outer-body experience. The younger me is on the grass, hurting and cowering. My black knight is charging towards the crowd, his intent very clear on his features. He sends them sprawling like bowling pins. The relief washes over me and he picks me up in his strong, firm grasp. His voice is soothing and his rapid fire questions are fully intent on finding out where I hurt. I promise him I'm fine and beg him to just take me home.

Bless him, he does. He carries me the whole way there. Not that it is too far, but I still weigh enough to be a burden. Angel doesn't seem to notice though and puts one foot in front of the other until he reaches my front door. Gently he lowers me to the ground so I can fish out my house keys from my pocket. I'm thankful my parents are both at work. He takes them from me and unlocks the door for me before he scoops me back up.

'Where do you want me to put you?'

'Upstairs, in my bedroom,' I whisper against his chest. I know I must look a mess, but I am even more shocked by my appearance when I catch sight of myself in the mirror on my wall.

I kick my shoes off and climb into bed, not caring that Angel is still standing in the room. I pull the covers over my head. There is a sob stuck in my chest just waiting to get out. There is enough fight left in me to keep it stuck right where it is, but the tears cannot be contained. Lying on my back, the hot wet tears start to stream down the sides of my face and run into my hair. Angel is still there. There are no words that I could say to him that would express my gratitude towards him.

'Bailey, honey?'

'Yeah,' I mumble from the sanctuary of the sheets.

'Let me see you. I need to check if you're okay.'

'No! I'm too ugly to look at right now.'

There is movement and then the sheets start to slowly peel off me; I cover my face with my hands to ward off his gaze. He takes up residence on my bed next to me and takes my hands in his, forcibly removing them from hiding my ensuing black eye and split lip.

'Look at me.' His voice is soft, warm, inviting, and commanding. It can't be helped. I do. There was nothing on this earth that would have prepared me for what I saw written quite plainly on his features. Love and adoration mixed with concern flip a switch inside of me. Any past notions of this man just went out the window. There was no bad reputation. No troubled past. Just him and me. Gently he wipes my tears.

'Thank you… for helping me.'

'Listen to me, Bailey. There is nothing I wouldn't do for you, you know? And you're not ugly – even with a black eye and cut lip. You're the most adorable, sweet, beautiful woman I have ever laid eyes on.'

His eyes are apprehensive and I can visibly see him holding his breath at this last remark. Angel's hand stills at the side of my face. I'm shocked. I didn't think he would ever feel this way about me. Ever. My expression must be quite readable, because he hurries to backtrack.

'I'm sorry, I know it's inappropriate.' His eyes dart away from mine as I stare him down.

'You think I'm beautiful?' There is no hesitation on his part.

'Yes.'

'Even like this?'

'Yes.' He licks his lips, a nervous reaction that makes *me* want to protect *him*. An urge comes over me like a wave sweeping over a rocky cliff – one that takes everything that is not secured back out with it into its depths. Sitting forward I reach for him, a brazenness I didn't know I possessed takes over as I grab his shirt and pull him towards me, crushing his lips to mine with abandon. This is my first kiss, and despite the pain I'm suffering, there is no way I'm ending it.

His tongue seeks out mine, an invisible line just crossed and now there is no turning back. There is a need between us that is calling to be fulfilled and we meet it head on. There is no roughness in his actions. His fingers dance across my clothes, light as feathers falling from a nest in the trees in spring. I'm captivated.

In the second his lips leave mine, I gaze upon his face. There is something angelic about him.

'Thank you for saving me, for being there. You're like my guardian angel you know.'

'Me? An angel?'

'Yes,' I nod firmly. 'You're definitely my angel. In fact, that's what I'm going to call you from now on – Angel.'

'You can't call a man Angel,' he says indignantly, although the corner of his lips pull up just a fraction to show that he is amused with it.

'Yes you can.' My voice is just a whisper, wanting to stand up to him, but not insult him. To me, it is so perfectly fitting. He strokes my face tenderly and kisses my lips ever so softly.

'Well okay. But only because it's you. If anyone else were to call me that I'd have to punch 'em on the nose.' I smile, happy that he's accepted my nickname so readily. His lips sweep back to mine and I fall back into the blissful induced haze while his fingers work their magic on my clothing.

The top part of my dress is first to go as he works it off my shoulders and down towards my hips. It hurts my ribs so bad, that I almost cry out loud. Instead I take short tiny breaths to curtail the consuming pain that is coming from within. There is no way I am going to stop him now.

Curiosity has the best of me. His head ducks to my neck and ever so slowly he kisses his hot mouth down towards my belly button, taking extra care as he trails over my ribs. My body is on fire. Not just from pain, but from passion too. All my senses are humming away and it is an exquisite balance of sensuality that I have never experienced before.

The disheveled dress I'm wearing slides easily down the rest of my body and off my legs. I say a silent prayer, thanking God that I shaved them just this morning. His tongue runs the length all the way to the edge of my panties. I'm shocked when I start to feel wet between my legs and am suddenly embarrassed that Angel will notice the wet spot on the fabric of my underwear. I move to cover myself with my hands, but he won't let me. He wants to see all of me.

'Don't cover yourself. You've nothing to be embarrassed about. Do you know how hot and hard you make me just by seeing that I make you wet?' There are no words as I don't think I have the maturity to say something appropriate. Instead I let him take them off. Only my bra remains now, but he doesn't move to touch it. Perhaps he thinks he will hurt me if he does. Bruise marks are already starting to spread across my torso, my pale skin not helping the obviousness of just having had the shit kicked out of me.

Angel takes off his clothes slowly, eager for me to watch his strip tease. His toned skin is evidence of his physical lifestyle. It bulges in all the right places, muscles rippling down his arms and across his stomach. Crawling up the bed towards me my heart starts to flutter. He is painstakingly slow and I like it. Here is a person I know well, but have never really seen. Everything about him now fills my sights.

He is sitting between my legs, waiting until I ache for him to be inside of me. His arms go to either side of my body, careful to hover over me without our skin touching. He knows he will hurt me if he puts any pressure on me at all, so instead he holds his weight, arm muscles flexed and strained.

'Can I make love to you?'

'You're asking me now?'

'I'll always get your permission first, nothing is assumed, Bailey.' I nod that I want him to. His eyes go wild with desire and yet his body still holds restrain. I'm pretty sure he knows I'm a virgin – hell, I think the whole school knows I'm a virgin. *But not for much longer.* My legs part willingly to accept him inside of me. His cock is big and I have a moment of panic, wondering how it will even fit inside of me. Ever so slowly he nudges it in.

The feeling is intense. On the one hand I want him to just shove it inside of me, but at the same time I have no desire to be hurt anymore. He pushes in further, testing the water as he goes. There is a point I begin to feel the tear and I gasp in pain as he nudges through it. I feel myself come apart around him and move my hips towards his. There must be some good endorphins coursing my body, because my other pain has ebbed to the background. Gently, gently he shifts inside of me.

Nothing has ever felt this good. His lips find mine once more and he kisses me until I taste blood. My lip has split open again and he gently licks the wound. Every single thing he's doing to me is blowing my mind. There isn't even enough space in my head to process everything that is happening. Instead I go with the flow. Soon I start to feel the build of sensation deep within my pussy. The more he strokes me with his cock, the greater the urge is for me to have him do it all the more.

'More,' I rasp. 'Please, more.'

He obeys and continues to stroke me, but never increases the pace.

In my dream, I am just about to come when I hear the seatbelt sign in the airplane go off and I start to wake from my perfectly crafted dream. With horror, I realize I am coming anyway, sitting right there amongst a plane full of people while my pussy starts to spasm. Outwardly I try to show none of the telltale signs that I have just enjoyed an orgasm. Beside me Carron is stretching, and I notice a little dribble at the corner of his mouth. He must too, because he wipes his face with the back of his hand. Cute, adorable Carron. But he will never be Angel.

Sitting there as our plane readies itself for landing in Astoria, I realize something. That was all it took. That one day I became his. Little did I know from that moment on Angel would do everything in his power to convince me that we shouldn't be together. I'm wondering, after our run-in over Christmas, if he's perhaps had a change of heart.

Thirteen

We unpack and put a load of washing on. Cooking dinner seems like too much of a chore so we order Italian takeout. While I finish off the laundry, Carron heads off to the neighbor's house to bring Jezebel home. In his absence, I am trying to concentrate on the task at hand, but my laptop is calling me from the kitchen bench. Contemplating for a second, I realize that I can't wait until I go to work tomorrow to check my email.

A mad dash to the front window and I fling back the curtains to spy on old Mrs. Phillips' house next door. Carron is at the front door chatting away. She could talk the ear off a donkey so I assume I am safe for the time being. Adrenalin surges through me as I race back to the kitchen and turn on the laptop. It hums to life immediately and I impatiently drum my fingers on the bench top while all the software runs through its startup process.

When asked for my user identification I quickly tap away at the keyboard and press enter. Instant internet connectivity sees me logging into my email account immediately. There on my screen is a little envelope icon, flashing away, pleasing me no end. It will be Angel for sure. I open it and am rewarded for my deceit.

To: bails@quickmail.com

From: thurmontlumberyard@wizzmail.net

Subject: Nothing's changed

… since that day. I still want, desire and need you. Fuck him off, I can't stand the thought of his paws on you a minute longer. We need to be together. Tell me what I need to do to make it happen.

Angel.

To: thurmontlumberyard@wizzmail.net

From: bails@quickmail.com

Subject: Show me you mean it…

What's changed? How can I believe that you won't just send me away again like you always do? You've always said we CANNOT be together. That there will always be consequences, ramifications for the past as well. So, now we can be together? How can I turn Carron away when you pushed me towards him in the first place? He's a kind man, Angel – does he deserve this? I know WE are fucked up, but I don't want to ruin another person's life because of our relationship. There has already been enough of that.

Bails xx

There are tears in my eyes. Although I want Angel more than anything in the world, I'm scared. Scared that he will change his mind once I finally let my heart have hope.

The back door swings open, bringing with it a gust of wind. I jump out of my skin, afraid I have been caught red handed doing something I shouldn't. Carron is all smiles and has Jezebel tucked firmly beneath his arm. He catches my expression.

'Hey, babe, everything okay? You look like you just saw a ghost.'

'No, I'm fine. You just scared the shit out of me is all.' I barely manage to choke out the words. Quickly I shut down the computer and block the screen with my body until it turns off.

'You're not doing work already are you?' Carron peers over my shoulder and I am thankful the screen chooses that moment to turn blank.

'Just a quick check of my email from work,' I lie.

'I don't know – workaholic you are.'

'You know me.'

'I sure do. Hey, did the restaurant say how long they would be?'

'About half an hour.'

'Great, in that case I'm gonna grab a shower before the food arrives.' He places Jezebel on the floor and kisses the top of my head.

'You're a bit hot, you feeling okay?'

'Sure.' *That's just the burn of deceit raging across my skin like a plague.*

'All right, back in a minute then.' His departure brings relief and I sag into a nearby chair. That was too close. I'm going to need to be more careful or I'm going to come awfully close to hurting a man who has only ever shown me kindness.

***

I have mixed feelings about returning to work. On the one hand I am busy, which makes me happy that I have something to take my mind off Angel and his last email to me. Unfortunately that only lasts as long as my computer remains silent. Every now and then there is a little ping noise coming from it, rudely interrupting my train of thought. My heartbeat quickens and I'm all nerves as I quickly click away to retrieve the mail, certain that it will be him.

It doesn't come and I'm beginning to feel that his absence of communication is his way of giving up on us. I dared to challenge him, and from the minute I pressed send on that email he has been quiet on the home front. My expectations must have risen. Normally in the past I would have accepted his lack of communication while he sorted his head out. Now I'm hurt more than ever. He gave me hope, and I was stupid enough to believe him for once. I sigh.

'That doesn't sound good.' Lyra has stopped clacking away at her keyboard and has her full attention directed at me.

'Rough week,' I explain.

'I thought you were supposed to enjoy Christmas; did you have a fight with Carron?' I almost snort with laughter. Me fighting with Carron? I have more chance of getting poked in the eye with a toothpick.

'Carron does not simply fight with anyone, he discusses. And no, we didn't have a fight.'

'Well something's up, you've got that "someone just ran over my puppy" look going on.'

'Do not,' I sulk.

'Do too. Tell you what, why don't you come out with me and the rest of the gang for a few drinks tonight? Carron's doing late shift anyway isn't he?'

'Yeah…'

'I can feel an excuse coming on and I'm not having any of it. You can damn well get your miserable ass out of the house for once and stop being a recluse.'

'I happen to like my own company, you know.'

'I'm sure you do, however you are still coming out tonight. Isn't that right, James?' she yells in his direction.

'Absolutely, no party poopers in this office.' He winks at me, as though we are sharing a secret. I scowl at them both before turning my attention back to the article I'm writing. Perhaps a little alcohol-induced happiness is just what the doctor ordered to dull the senses.

By late afternoon I have managed to switch my mood around and am actually a little excited about the prospect of going out on a week night. I even forget about checking my email every five minutes to see if Angel has messaged me. My cell beeps in my bag next to my desk and I retrieve it to see who the text is from.

Carron's message is short and sweet. He's going to be working a couple of extra hours in the ER to cover for a friend and shouldn't be home until around 2:00 a.m. I send him a message back letting him know that I'm going out for drinks with the gang from work and will catch a cab home from the bar downtown.

'You ready to head off?' asks Lyra. I check my watch and can't believe it's after 5:00 p.m. already.

'Sure, just let me grab my coat.' The four of us close up the office and decide to walk to a bar located down near the Astoria Riverfront Trolley. The place has been there since 1926 and still has most of its charm from when it was first built. The locals call it Asti's Two, because once upon a time it was only one of two bars that served the city's alcohol. The actual name of the bar is something boring like Danny's – but no one from around here ever calls it that.

We all settle ourselves around a table that faces the waterfront and Jenna pulls the short straw to buy the first round of drinks. Instead of complaining, she smirks. There is an unwritten rule that whenever the four of us go out for a round, we each take turns in buying. The only problem is you are not allowed to pick what you want to drink. Instead you have to down whatever the buyer brings back to the table. I swear I have gotten sick more times than I care to remember from following these stupid rules.

While Jenna gets the drinks, James trots off to order some hot cheesy fries sprinkled with paprika and black pepper. There aren't many patrons at this hour, but I know by the time we leave the place will be packed.

'So how's Sean?' I am referring to Lyra's latest squeeze who she met while on a trip to Baltimore recently.

'I wouldn't know, we broke up.' There is no emotion at all in her voice and she is checking out the few would be suitors that are already filling their glasses with lager.

'Sorry, Lyra, why didn't you tell me?'

'Do I look upset?'

'Actually, no.'

'That's because I'm not. There wasn't much to tell really. He was a little young for me and was falling waaaay too hard. I just want to have fun, you know? Besides – he lived so far away there wasn't any point when he's not here to fuck my pussy.'

'Lyra!' My hiss draws the stares of patrons nearby who seem suddenly interested in our animated discussion.

'Don't be melodramatic, Bailey. I'm a woman, he's a man. We have needs you know.' She's talking to me like I'm a grade-schooler and I have no idea what adult relationships are really about.

'I meant keep it down! I'm sure the whole bar just heard your comment. Frankly I don't care who you fuck,' I whisper.

'Oh don't be such a prude, Bails. Everybody in this room is having sex – well maybe except for you. You seem a little uptight lately. Is Carron not any good in the bedroom?'

'Don't be stupid. He's perfectly... fine.' This conversation is getting way off track. 'Anyway, what makes you think I'm uptight?'

'I've known you, what? Five years? I think I would be the first person to know if my best friend is a little tenser than usual. I'm very perceptive like that.' She sniffs as though she is deeply offended, although I know it's just an act.

'There's nothing wrong with me,' I sigh, knowing I would have to do more and say more than that for her to be convinced. Thankfully we are saved any further uncomfortable discussion when James returns to join us. He sits next to me and puts our number on the wood table.

'Do you remember Hamish, Bailey?'

'Hamish?' He stares me down intently, as though I have suddenly grown two antlers with jingly bells on them.

'Yeah, Hamish. He used to play with us when we were little. You remember that summer you visited and we all decided to go down the hill on my go-kart and we all came off? He broke his arm...' He's still waiting, but his tone is getting impatient.

'Oh, yes. Dark hair right?'

'Yeah, that's right. Well he's going to be back in town tonight. I told him you'd be here too and that we'd be going out for drinks. He seemed pretty excited to see you again, if you know what I mean.' James is just about killing himself with laughter as he waggles his eyebrows at me.

'Very funny. I'm with Carron you know.'

'Sure, sure. But there's nothing like hooking back up with old friends is there?'

'I guess not.' I look around, trying to pick faces out of the crowd of people that linger near the bar.

'Don't mind her,' smirks Lyra. 'She's got her panties in a twist over something.'

'I told you I am completely fine.' On the inside though, I am far from it.

Fourteen

We are soon joined by Jenna who holds a tray with our drinks on it. I'm almost afraid to look and see what she has bought for us. Placing the tray on the table she smiles a triumphant smile.

'Ta da! Apple martinis!' Most people would be excused for thinking Jenna is a wallflower. To be honest she looks a little like me, although her hair is mousey brown not flaming auburn. She wears a funky pair of specs and dresses in retro skirts and knee high boots that look like something a librarian from the 1970s would wear. Even her hair is piled on her head in a bun. But that is where you would draw the line in similarities. Take off the clothes and you would get an idea of the girl that lives inside her body. She has funky tats over a lot of her skin and she favors the odd piercing or two. In this weather with her body wrapped up in cardigans and the like you'd be hard pressed seeing them.

'Oh shit, really? Apple martinis? You remember how sick I was last time I drank those, don't you?' James whines something fierce when he wants to.

'Yes, as a matter of fact I do. Cheers.' Jenna grins at him mischievously. He groans as he takes his offering from the tray.

'Fine,' he grumbles, 'but don't say I didn't warn you.' He takes his first sip and looks like he has just swallowed a bitter pill. We all follow suit and soon settle into our groove of drinking, dancing, toilet, repeat. By eleven o'clock I am completely smashed. I've consumed ten beverages – all with high alcohol content, danced my ass off with the guys and consumed a huge portion of cheesy fries. My stomach feels awfully sloshy and I try desperately not to throw up as I take myself to the bathroom for the hundredth time.

The others are still dancing while I make my way to the ladies' room that is located down a long corridor that passes the kitchen. The smell of food wafts out at me and my stomach twists in response. Right about now I am wishing I stopped drinking about two hours ago. The floor starts to spin and I brace myself against the wall and let the coolness of its surface touch my cheeks. Behind me a voice startles me.

'You okay?' I whip around. Oh my god. The sight of him is sobering to say the least.

'Angel? Why are you here?'

'I told you, whatever it takes. Seriously, are you okay right now?' So this is why he never answered my email. He must have caught a flight out this morning.

'I just feel a little ill is all. I think... I think I'm gonna be sick!' The urge to vomit pushes at the top of my esophagus and my cheeks flush with heat. I push past him into the men's room as I know there is no way I will make it to the ladies'. He follows me in as I seek out a stall and hang my head over the bowl.

I'm only mildly embarrassed that he is watching me wretch all over the porcelain bowl. That's the beauty of knowing Angel for so long: he's seen me in worse situations.

In fact, he was the one who took me drinking for the first time in my life and got me so rotten drunk I couldn't walk straight. Pondering this as I empty my stomach, I realize that Angel has been the one person in my life who has always been there for a lot of my firsts.

As my convulsing stops I slowly rise and reach for the toilet paper to blow my nose and clear my throat. I can feel a bit of cheesy fry stuck in the back of my throat and hack unceremoniously to get it out.

'Nice, Bails.'

'Sorry.' I'm sheepish to say the least. Not a very nice welcome to town for him I'm sure. I turn to face the mirror and am mortified by my reflection. My eyes are bloodshot and my hair hangs limply, sweaty and damp from all the dancing I have been doing.

'A little old to be getting drunk, aren't we?'

'Well I might not have been so inclined to drown my sorrows if you didn't keep making me miserable,' I snap.

'I make you miserable?' I've hurt his feelings terribly with one little sentence uttered out of my mouth.

'No,' I sigh, 'of course not.'

'Why say that then?' His eyes trail me as I make my way to the sink and splash water on my face. I rinse my mouth for good measure before searching for a breath mint in my handbag strapped around my shoulder.

'Because I freaking missed you and I haven't heard a word from you since I sent you the email.' My words are slightly slurred and I wonder if this is why he doesn't seem to understand me. He spreads his arms wide, complete lack of comprehension etched across his features.

'This is me showing you, Bails. I caught the first available flight out, and I mean for you to make a choice.' Just then the bathroom door to the men's room swings open and a large bellied biker comes swaying in. He gives us the once over before entering the last cubicle on the left.

'Come on.' He takes my hand and pulls me from the bathroom. Back in the hallway, the music from the live band filters down to us. The place is just starting to come alive. I'm sure if I left now that the others would be too intoxicated to put up too much of a fight if I took my leave for the night.

'I'll need to let the guys know that I am leaving – I can't just walk out you know.'

'Go ahead. I'll take the back door and meet you out the front. I've got a rental car waiting.' I nod and take off for the front of the bar. Lyra is bumping pelvises with a young guy that looks like he's barely legal, although admittedly he is one fine piece of ass, even for her. Jenna and James are getting their grove on too, and now that my mind is a little clearer since I emptied my guts, there seems to be a little bit of chemistry floating between the two.

Knowing Lyra the best out of the three, I approach her first and signal I need to talk to her. Mr. Barely Legal takes the opportunity to grab a drink while I let her know that I am on my way home.

'But, Bails, honey, the party's just getting started!' she argues while her glazed eyes shine in the light.

'I'll leave you guys to it. I'm bushed and I've already puked my guts up in the bathroom.'

'Oh ewie! That is totally gross, Bailey Michaels. Don't you dare breathe any of your sick breath on me.' She takes a step backwards as though in doing so she will avoid my stink breath. I roll my eyes and wave goodbye. I don't want to interrupt James and Jenna, so I wave to them from the edge of the dance floor. James catches sight of me and twirls Jenna towards me.

'You're not leaving are you?' James is out of breath from the dancing and I can see his chest heaving under his tight fitting shirt.

'I'm beat and feel sick. I'll see you guys tomorrow.'

'But Hamish hasn't even turned up yet!'

'Some other time.' I shrug my shoulders, as if to say 'it can't be helped'.

'You're one big party pooper. Later, Bails.' They both blow me a kiss as they head back into the sea of people now cramming the dance floor.

Stepping out into the cool air brings me one step closer to feeling more sober. Headlights come towards me from the rear car park and I can see Angel's outline behind the wheel. He pulls in tight near the front door and I jump into the passenger seat.

'Ready?'

'Yeah, where are we going?'

'Is Carron at your place?'

'No, he's working until 2:00 a.m.'

'Then that's where we're going.' He checks his watch to make note of the time.

'Seriously, Angel, what are you doing here? You know you can't be seen about town.'

'I don't give a shit anymore, Bails. All I want is you. All I've ever wanted is you, and let's face it – you're just as fucking miserable without me as I am without you.'

'Maybe… but that doesn't change the fact that we could never go out in public together.' I spy his profile while I'm talking to him. There is something I'm looking for. Perhaps I am searching for signs of regret or upset over this fact, but his features remain calm and retrospective.

'That doesn't matter to me. I've lived that life, and believe me it blows. I can't stand these little snippets of you here and there. I want you, all of you, and I'm not taking no for an answer.'

My breath catches in my throat. I have waited so long for him to say those words to me that suddenly I'm panicking and questioning if it is what I really want. I know deep down that I do, and I realize that my panic is at the thought of breaking Carron's heart. Despite my love for Angel, I really don't want to hurt him in this way.

'You're really ready to live in secrecy the rest of our lives and accept that we will never be a couple around people we love?'

'It will be hard, sure. But there will never be anyone who I love more than you. It's always been you, Bailey. Only you. Please come away to live with me.' All I needed was the diamond ring and I think my long-term fantasy would be complete.

'What about work?' He takes his eyes off the road to glance at me.

'You're kidding right? You have a laptop. Most of your work is done on there, right?'

'Sure, but I would still need approval from my boss.'

'Well get it!' He's beginning to get exasperated from all the walls I am starting to put up.

'What about my house? And Carron?' He ponders for a second while he navigates through the streets towards my house.

'Rent it out – to Carron. Two birds with one stone, Bails.' He chuckles heartily at this and I slap his arm roughly.

'Ow! What the hell was that for?'

'You know damn well what that was for! How can you be so cold towards him when you pushed me into his arms in the first place?'

'I never told you to go through with it. You had a choice you know.' His mood has turned dark and his jaw muscles clench at the side.

'You inconceivable shit! Everything I have ever done is because I fucking love you! Don't you dare sit there and judge me. You've got no idea what it is like to love someone so much and yet they repeatedly reject you and tell you everything about your relationship is wrong.' My anger is rearing her wicked head big time and my body starts to shake as the adrenalin takes over. Angel has me well and truly pissed and tears start to sting my eyes. I choke back a sob as I stare out the car window, only mildly distracted by the rain drops that have started to pool on the front windscreen.

'Aww fuck, Bails, don't cry sweetheart. I'm not blaming you, really. To be honest I'm just so goddamn pissed with myself. I shouldn't have let you be with him. It hurts too damn much to even think about you together. I don't want to make you cry or feel bad about it. I just want it to change is all.' His hand reaches out for my thigh and he strokes my leg with his free hand while he steers the car with the other.

'I do too, and of course I want to be with you. It's just a lot for us to talk about tonight and Carron will be home soon. There's no way you can be at the house when he gets home, okay?'

'I know that. When I saw you leave work you looked so glum that I just had to follow you and make sure you were okay. I'm staying at the local motel, but I just needed to hold you once and have you tell me that you'll come and visit me this weekend so that we can talk this through. Can you do that?'

'That would involve lying to Carron, but I suppose that's nothing unusual for the likes of us who seem to be morally challenged.' Angel knows I am being facetious and grins at me in the confines of the darkened cab of the car.

'Shall I take that as a yes then?' I decide it is best to put us both out of our misery.

'Aye, that's a yes.' I say this in my best Scottish accent, one to rival the actors in *Braveheart*. Having got what he came for, Angel is now quiet and content with the silence that passes between us. He swings the rental car into my driveway and turns off the engine.

'What are you doing? You can't come in you know, Carron will be home from work soon.'

'I'll just be a minute,' he promises.

'Really? Like literally one minute?'

'Well, maybe two… or three – but no more than ten.' My raised eyebrows give him cause to further explain himself. 'I just want to tuck you in is all.'

'No sex?'

'Don't fucking tempt me. I promise, a goodnight kiss is all I want.'

'Okay, let's hurry.' We exit the car and rush out of the rain to the front porch. I'm still a bit wobbly on my legs, but manage to fumble my keys out of my bag and get the lock undone. Angel follows me in and bolts the lock behind us. I grab his hand in the dark and lead him towards the stairs in the back of the house. He follows obediently to the upstairs master bedroom.

I make him sit on the edge of the bed as I slip into the bathroom to brush my teeth and throw a night shirt on. When I come out he's waiting for me, his eye all gleaming with desire.

'Don't get any ideas. You really need to be going,' I say as I climb under the sheets, the physical barrier of the material not really posing any threat that could possibly keep us apart. Only his silhouette is visible as he approaches me, but the sight is so familiar that it's almost like a million light bulbs are shining on him and I can see every single line, hair and mark on his face.

God I want this man. Right now. But I know time is running out.

'Kiss me quick,' I hasten him.

'No, I want to kiss you slow.'

'There's no time,' I plead.

'There will always be time for one last kiss.' He dips his head slowly and takes my lips full in his mouth. His tongue is warm as it probes deep inside my mouth. He kisses me with such passion my pussy starts to ache for him. I wrap my arms around his neck and greedily pull him to me, wanting every inch of him on me. We kiss deeply and passionately, time suddenly taking absence of this moment. He finally pulls apart from my grip and quickly kisses my forehead.

'I have to go.'

'You always do,' I say miserably. I never should have kissed him, it was idiotic of me to think that I could do it without wanting more.

'No fair. This time it's not my fault.'

'I know, I'm just being a bitch because I want you to stay.'

'Well you can be a bitch all you like then.' With a final graze of my lips he stands to leave.

'Goodnight, Bailey. I'll see you on the weekend, okay?' His whispers reach me as his hand finds the door knob. Already my eyes are closing, the need for sleep dominating my body without my permission to do so.

'Can you lock the door please, Angel?'

My mumbles must reach him because he says, 'Of course, Bails. I love you.' The last of his words touch me as I feel his presence being dragged away from me. As I slip into a deep sleep I am yelling those words back to him. *I love you too, Angel. Always.*

Sleep descends, bringing with it a distant memory. I don't often think of it, but sometimes it pushes through to my dreams unbidden. It's always black and white though, like I'm watching an old movie. A younger me walks the hallways of school. I walk guardedly – there is still so much pain. Only a week has passed since I had the shit beaten out of me and my body still bears the effects. My parents were told I fell off my bike. They never questioned my honesty. I had never given them reason to.

In my dream the other students are absent. Even though I know in reality they were all about that day, their eyes on me – judging, whispering and gossiping. The linoleum floor squeaks under the rubber soles of my shoes. It's been raining. I pass the last row of lockers in the hallway and the door on the left opens.

My eyes flit from the name plaque on the door to the face that accompanies it. Coach Sawyer looks shocked to see me, but there is no avoiding him now.

'Bailey.' His tone is warm, comforting. He's sweaty, the wet patches on his pale grey shirt indicating he has just been doing something physical. He notices me looking at him and I blush and turn my gaze away.

'We just had track and field,' he offers as a way of explanation.

'Uh-huh.' *What an idiot I am! Stop staring!*

'Have you got a minute?' He scans the hallway before stepping back to invite me into his office. I follow him in and take a seat at his desk. He closes the door behind us, intimating that our conversation is for our ears only. He takes a moment to sweep his eyes over my body and I suddenly feel naked under his stare. Perhaps this was not such a good idea.

'Did you need to speak to me?'

He looks perplexed for a minute.

'I know it's been a rough week for you.' My breath sucks in. We really can't have this conversation here. I won't go there. Not now.

'I'm fine.' My tone is flat. It cuts him off.

'Bailey, I... uh, I just need to know you are doing okay...'

'Thanks, but you know I am. I'll catch you in gym class this afternoon.' I get up abruptly and leave him lost for words as I disappear back into the bowels of the school building. I never meant for him to see me at the mercy of bullies. For better or worse though, he cares. This has always stayed with me, that another human being cares for me, Bailey Michaels. As I dream the night away, his face comes and goes, haunting me with the memories I'd sometimes rather forget.

Fifteen

I have become very good at lying to Carron. In fact, I'm appalled at the level of trust he has in me. It's Thursday night, and I am yet to inform him that I will be away for the weekend. With another man no less. I'm sure if he knew he would be more than upset. *Shocked* and *disbelief* are words that spring to mind.

For once he has a night off and he's suggested we make some tacos with homemade salsa while sipping on a Cabernet Sauvignon I picked up on my way home from work. It's cozy in the kitchen. The little pot belly stove in the corner of the room is doing its job nicely and warming the air in the room. The cat is encircling herself around my legs, patiently waiting for scraps of food that might fall her way. Carron prepares the meat while I continue to chop vegetables.

'How was your day?' I ask, already knowing full well where this conversation is going to end up.

'Great! I got to go fishing this morning, and then had a quick lunch with Eddy at the grill before topping it all off with football on the couch this afternoon.'

'Sounds like your kind of day.'

'Yeah, I kind of needed the time off, especially since I'm rostered to work right through from tomorrow till Tuesday.'

'That's hardly fair,' I offer. To be honest I'm thrilled, but it wouldn't do to be openly excited about it.

'Yeah, but it's money in the pocket and it won't be for too much longer. The hospital is having a reshuffle of staff so we can cope with the increasing demand for patient care. And you know me; I never knock back a cry for help when it's needed.' He smiles so kindly at me then I just about die.

I'm entranced by his face, as though seeing him for the first time since we first got together. His hair is longer, and he has it tied up at the back today. The stubble on his chin is still there and tonight he has his glasses on, endearing me to him all the more. Empathy is not something I allow Carron, because he is mine – to be here for me when I need him. It was me who cried for his help when we first got together, wanting someone to take my mind off Angel. He did that without even knowing it. To be fair to him, I'm going to have to call off the engagement.

Whether Angel goes through with 'us' or not, I can't ruin Carron's chance at happiness for the sake of my own selfishness. I try to avoid his eyes as my own start to tear up. I have to stop chopping the vegetables because my blurry eyesight is going to get me my finger chopped off if I'm not careful. My mood change doesn't go unnoticed by Carron.

'Hey, Bailey Boo, what's up honey?' I stifle a sob at his sincerity and concern.

'Nothing, it's just the onions.'

'Bullshit.' He grins at me. 'You're like the only person in the world who I know that does not get teary when she cuts onions. It's like an in-built super human power or something.' The grin stays on his face, but uncertainty shrouds his eyes.

'Really, I'm okay,' I sniffle. God, I really need to get my shit together.

'You're not all right, come here.' He grabs my hand and puts the knife down on the bench, the cat scattering from under my feet. Carron pulls me towards the little arm chair that sits next to the pot belly stove and eases down into it, dragging me into his big safe arms as he does. He cuddles me close, letting me bury my head against his chest while he holds me. I start to cry for real. Big chest racking sobs that make me sound hysterical. His body is tense underneath me, but I ignore his discomfort. He's killing me with kindness and I have no way of stopping the little selfish girl inside who needs to have her tears dried. His big warm hand strokes my back and eventually I'm silenced into nothingness.

'Bails, Bails, Bails. You can talk to me, honey. I know there are things about your past that you have never really wanted to share with me, but you can talk to me you know?'

'Uh-huh,' I hiccup.

'Seriously, I hate seeing you upset. It's not me is it?'

'No.' And there it is: the Satan spawn side of my personality that rears her ugly head. I try commanding myself to tell him the truth, but that big bit of sawdust at the back of my throat prevents me from uttering a single word.

'Well there must be something bothering you… is it the wedding?'

'No.' *Liar!* I scream at myself, for I know I can never see us walking down the aisle together.

'I wish you'd open up to me, Bailey. I really want to help you if I can.' Man oh man. If I told him this dirty little secret he would run for the hills for sure. There would then be nothing I could do to stop his loathing for me. I dry my tears and pull myself together. I'm not at all surprised, but the words *villainous bitch* sing-song about my head.

'I'm okay, Carron, really. It's just been a long week and I'm tired. To top it all off work is sending me away to do a spread for this month's issue which leaves me really pressed for time to get it in by the deadline.' Right now, I am super thankful that Carron has no interest in fashion magazines. Sports yes, fashion – forget it. And so continues my web of deceit.

'Oh, Bails, that's too bad honey. Would you like me to take the weekend off and come with you? We could have a nice romantic getaway while you're at it.'

'No!' He's just as surprised by my outburst as I am, and I have to admit I didn't quite mean to come across as vehemently as I did. 'I mean, no. Thank you though. Danzar is going for the whole industrial background look for the clothing brand and they are going to shoot in Chicago which won't be very romantic.' Wow, sometimes the callous bitch that lives inside of me surprises even me.

'Are you sure? Because I could ask if my boss can get someone to cover for me.'

'Really, I'm sure.'

'I would ask for you, you know that right?'

'Sure I do. I don't know what I do to deserve you.' I kiss the top of his head as I hop off his lap to go and get a tissue. Shaky breaths rattle away in my chest as I urge myself to calm down. Sometimes I feel I am so close to spilling my secret that if someone gives me half an inch to spill my guts then I'm sure I would never shut up. Confession would take all winter.

Nose blown and demeanor back intact, I wash my hands in the kitchen sink and resume cutting the vegetables at the bench. Carron is back at the stove stirring the mince as it cooks.

'So, when's your flight?' His tone is light, casual, engaging. I'm instantly on high alert because I am suspicious that he is skeptical of my story.

'Just after lunch tomorrow.'

'Are you going to take a cab?'

'Yeah, the company will pick up the tab.' We continue to make small talk over dinner and I admittedly have a little too much wine. In my inebriated state my sorrow and remorse over lying to Carron starts to eat me alive. To me, only one thing will result from my weekend away with Angel. Upon my return I know I'm going to have to leave Carron. That is if I actually have the guts to tell him it's over. Even my subconscious is doubting herself.

After dinner we retire to the living room. The exhaustion of the day and the tears from crying earlier leave my eyelids heavy. I struggle to keep them open but know I am fighting a losing battle. Carron notices and flicks off the television. With ease he scoops me into his arms and he carries me up the flight of stairs to the bedroom.

Gently he undresses me and I am too numb to care. He puts me in bed and starts to caress my skin, starved to be touched, just not by him. But I do love him, don't get me wrong. I'm just not in love with him. Another stole my heart a long time ago. But my guilt rides my back, admonishing me to be kind and receptive to him. Another part of my brain tells me to stop being such pushover. But sweet Bailey always wins out when it comes to Carron. So I open up my legs to him, encouraging him to dive into the depths of my despair.

Carron sighs with contentment and I wish I weren't so spoiled, like a rotting apple that is bad all the way to the core. We actually have the best sex we have ever had, but I know that is because in a way I am saying goodbye to him tonight. When I get back, I know that it won't be long before I will leave him to be with Angel all the time. To finally live my life the way I have dreamed since I was just fifteen years old. We both cry out as we orgasm and tears slide down my face.

I'm so sorry, Carron. So, so sorry. Please forgive me. Please, I need you to forgive me for what I am about to do to you.

Sixteen

Without having to get up early for work, I sleep off my night of wine-fuelled indulgence. I finally stir when I feel Jezebel clawing me with her talons, a clear sign that I have slept well past her breakfast time. Groaning I roll over onto my back and let my eyes slowly peel open.

'Stop it Jez! I'm coming, okay?' She pays me no attention and keeps up with her tirade. I notice the empty bed beside me and wonder where Carron is. He wasn't supposed to start work until later in the day, but there is a note there on his pillow. I reach over and grab it.

Bailey, I loved making love to you last night. For the first time I feel like you really let yourself go with me. I need to see this girl more, she makes me smile. I've gone fishing with Eddy before work, so I will miss your departure, but I wanted you to know I have never loved you more. Whatever you need from me, whenever you need it, I will always be here to give it to you. See you when you get back. Call me if you get a spare minute, okay? Yours, Carron.

I fold the note and clutch it to my chest. The lump in my throat refuses to dislodge despite how many times I swallow. For the millionth time I question my sanity and all that I am doing. But despite my guilt, my love or any other emotion that is connected with Carron, it will never override anything I feel for Angel. So I place the note from him into my bathrobe pocket and head downstairs to get breakfast.

The cat follows, eager to get her share too. I settle for strong black coffee with a healthy dollop of thickened cream and set about making eggs and toast. I don't have long to get ready. There is still my suitcase to pack and my flight actually leaves earlier than I told Carron.

A call is placed to the taxi company before I head back upstairs to shower. I let the hot water run over my skin and knead out the tension that has built in my shoulders. Stepping out onto the bathmat I finally feel relaxed enough to start getting excited about my impending visit with Angel. My cheeks involuntarily flush at the memories of our last love making in the hotel and I know that he will devour me again with the same expertise. He has always known just how to press my buttons.

I carefully select my clothing, knowing that Angel's need to touch my skin will only be hindered by pants and underwear. The long wool skirt I select is accompanied by opaque pantyhose, the chill outside a little much, even for me. A white turtleneck finishes off my ensemble and I add the thin gold chain Angel gave me for my nineteenth birthday.

Pushing thoughts of Angel to the side I quickly throw an overnight bag together. Jeans, two sweaters, underwear for three days and my toiletries kit should just about do it. Travelling light means that I can skip the luggage turnstile at the other end.

Back in the kitchen I change the kitty litter and place fresh water and food for the cat on the floor. I grab a paper and pencil and quickly scrawl a note to Carron.

Carron

Thank you for being such a kind and wonderful man. I hope you enjoy your weekend and I will call you later today. Have fun while I'm gone and please don't worry about me. Sorry for last night, I'm rather embarrassed that I was such a baby, but I tend to get a little emotional when I'm tired. See you soon, Bailey.

I place a lipstick kiss on the bottom of the paper and secure it on the kitchen table under a vase that holds flowers Carron bought for me last week. Knowing the taxi will be here shortly, I decide to wait on the front porch in the rocking chair. No sooner do I get outside than the taxi pulls up, parking tight against the curb. I grab my jacket and bag and make my way down the short flight of stairs.

The taxi driver is not up for small talk, which suits me because neither am I. My whole brain is consumed with one focus: Angel. This is not the first time I have been to his home, but usually we meet when I am out of town on business. Normally even this takes him a lot of convincing. He has always been so intent on hiding our love, that in the past when I have headed out to Thurmont it has always been under the secrecy of nightfall, smuggled in like a prisoner – except I go of my own free will. While the taxi speeds past familiar landmarks in Astoria, I wonder what it would be like to leave here, to move and live with Angel. Would I be happy? Would he? Or would his guilt make him send me away again? I couldn't bear the thought of that.

Once was bad enough; I stopped eating for weeks until he came to his senses and promised me we would continue with our fucked up affair. Only it wasn't fucked up to me. It was perfect. I have never dared believe that we could actually have a relationship where we would be with each other every day as a couple. Until now.

The cab pulls up outside of the airport terminal and I hand over some bills to pay the driver. Grabbing my bags, I jump out and head inside to check in. Seriously, I'm like a kid in a candy shop. My excitement bubbles from the top of my shoulders all the way down to where it pools at my feet. If I didn't care about looking stupid I probably would have skipped inside like a gleeful grade-schooler.

The poised brunette behind the counter accepts my driver's license and my flight confirmation print out. I watch as her long manicured fingers tap away at the buttons on her keyboard.

'Any luggage you will be checking in today?'

'No, I just have my carry-on.'

'Okay then Ms. Michaels, you're seated in row D4. You can now make your way through security and then head to gate five.'

'Thanks,' I say and she nods, handing me my boarding pass.

'Have a good flight.' I head off through security and clear it no problems. Well of course I would. I'm an adulterer, not a terrorist. There is still a bit of a wait before boarding so I grab a coffee and park my ass in a seat near the big glass windows that afford me a view over the runway. My phone vibrates and I hear the doorbell sound effect I have set for when I receive new text messages. It's from Lyra.

I don't know why you had to piss off to Chicago so quickly, but let me tell you, missy, I'm not entirely comfortable with covering for you! When you get back, you and I are going to have a little chat. I mean it!

Bitch. Some friend she is. I mean, why does she have to get all high and mighty with me? Having her message me is a serious mood killer, only because it reminds me to be guilty when I otherwise would be thrilled to bits. Deciding to placate her rather than ignore or antagonize, I send her a message back.

Thank you for being a good friend. You know I wouldn't have asked if it wasn't important. Will go for drinks when I get back – my shout.

There is only a brief second before the doorbell on my phone chimes out again.

Fine! Okay, already. But you know I'm here if you wanna spill your guts right?

My reply is short and sweet.

I do! <3 U. Talk later xx

While my phone is out I decide to send a text to Carron as well.

Boarding soon. Will call you from the other end. Have a great time fishing. X

As I slide my phone back into my handbag the loud speaker in the terminal goes off, announcing that my flight is just about to start boarding. I throw my empty coffee cup in the trash and stand with the rest of the passengers who also cannot wait five minutes to allow the surge of people to pass before they take their turn at the gate. My turn to hand over my ticket arrives.

'I hope your trip to Hagerstown is a pleasant one, ma'am.'

'Thank you.' My reply gets lost as I am pushed forward by the sea of people behind me. Angel will be picking me up from Hagerstown, a neighboring town near Thurmont.

Not long now and I will be in his arms again. While boarding the plane, I try not to let out a little squeal of glee.

Seventeen

The minute I step through the departure doors I see him.
We only have eyes for each other. His dark hair has been cut
short but it's still spiky at the front. Warm brown eyes meet
mine and then skim down the rest of my body, drinking me
in as they go. Just his look alone turns me to jelly and I have
to force myself to place one leg in front of the other. When I
reach him my nose instantly picks up his scent, his aftershave
enlightening my senses and arousing my soul.

'Hey, Bails.' His voice trickles over me like warm honey.
It's rich and sexy. All I want him to do is talk to me all day
with that voice of his.

'Hi, Angel.' I graze his cheek with a quick kiss, knowing
full well that we normally do not indulge in public displays
of affection, but being quite unable to restrain myself from
making some kind of contact with him.

'You packed light.' The tone in his voice has switched to
disapproving and I am anxious that I have already put a foot
wrong.

'You know I'm just here for the weekend this time,' I
whisper above the throng of the airport chatter.

'We'll see about that.' My carry-on is snatched out of my
grasp and he slings it over his shoulder with ease. He takes
my hand in his big warm one and stuffs both of them in his
oversized jacket pocket. It is a tartan print lined with real

sheep's wool. Today he really does look like a wood cutter. His hand is hard and calloused from all the outdoor labor, but it is warm and familiar. My mind runs off, remembering all the places it has touched on my body. Angel is completely unaware of the effect he is having on me as he leads me out into the bitter cold that is north Maryland in the winter.

His usual car is not here. There is too much snow on the ground so he has brought his company's truck from the lumber yard to use instead. Angel opens my door for me and uses a well-placed hand on my rear to boost me up into the cab. I grin from ear to ear like a school girl, glad that the prettiest boy is giving me affection. His grin is just as wide, and I watch through the front windscreen as he trots around to the driver's side. People shouldn't be allowed to look as good as Angel does. It's damn well distracting.

He cranks the ignition key over and the engine hums to life. The windscreen wipers are on a slow setting, dusting the snowflakes that are falling from the sky away from his line of sight. Once we have exited the car park his hand leaves the stick shift and seeks out mine in my lap. His touch is electric and I am having a hard time resisting my need to pounce on him. We drive in comfortable silence towards his log cabin in Thurmont.

I don't recognize the roads or landscape as easily as I do in Astoria, but I pay more attention this trip around. If I'm going to move here to be with Angel then I will need to be able to navigate my way around the place. Here is really the only place we can be open with our love for one another. Here I could have a new identity.

Off country Manahan Road, Angel swings the truck onto a gravel driveway bordered by a large wooden fence on either side. To the right is a huge sign, indicating the property is home to his lumber yard. He continues past the mill and machinery to the road just behind where all the lumber is stored. It takes us through a densely wooded forest that is part of the hundred or so hectares he owns. We drive for a while at a snail's pace until the vegetation starts to thin out. In the distance a clearing forms at the end of the road and I glimpse the log cabin Angel built by hand.

There's a shed attached to the side of the house, and I know from previous visits that all of his machinery and tools are stored in there. A short flight of steps leads to a wrap-around verandah. He has several potted plants and comfortable furniture to relax on so one can enjoy the outdoors. It is a small cabin, but functional and utterly charming. The roof is shingled with oak tiles and the chimney flue poking out of the top is spilling out smoke. Around the rear of the house is more of the dense woodland that we just passed through. It frames the house and gives it a Hansel and Gretel feel.

Angel turns the ignition off and the instantaneous silence is deafening. We turn to look at each other and it's all over. No longer can we restrain ourselves from each other. Too long emotions have been held back and now that we are in the middle of our own private sanctuary there is nothing that will keep us apart.

I fling myself at him, lips locking with his and my hands gripping his jaw. He groans with pleasure and slides his tongue in my mouth, seeking out my own. We kiss like teenagers in love, and in a way I feel like one again. Every moment we get to spend like this I am transported back to the first time we made love when I was just a teenager. It feels like yesterday, but my love for Angel has far surpassed the desire and emotion we had for each other in the beginning.

He breaks away from me for the briefest of seconds and I am left dazed, unsure why he has stopped kissing me. Bending forward he reaches for the leaver that slides his seat the whole way back.

'Come 'ere,' he growls once he is back in position. I scramble over the gear column and straddle his lap. His hands fist my long hair and he pulls my lips to his so that he can consume me. Heaven – I am in absolute heaven. Angel has the softest lips, despite the fact he has a small amount of stubble that covers his face. Our passionate kisses become needy and I know what is coming next. In my teenage years we spent many a night making love in his car. We could go anywhere, anytime and hide from the rest of the world. No one ever knew what we were up to.

One night he drove me all the way to Philadelphia just to see an art exhibit I had been dying to see. It was a romantic and sweet gesture that I think about often. While browsing the gift shop there he had surprised me by buying me a mood ring. It was a tacky souvenir, but I loved it all the same because it was from him. He slid it on my finger and joked that this way he would always be able to tell when I was hot for him. Over time, I wore it so much the cheap metal wore thin and snapped. To this day I still keep it in a box, locked away with other mementos that remind me of our time together.

He transports me back to the present when his hands leave my hair and skim my shoulder blades, tracing their way around to my breasts. They do not stop there though. Circling my waist he pulls my hips downwards so that my pelvis crushes his. He grinds against me, thrusting his erection hard up towards my pussy. His hands start to shove my wool skirt up towards my hips. I'm wearing stockings, but this is a mere inconvenience to Angel. He momentarily stops with the feverish kissing so his eyes can take in my undergarments.

There is no way he is letting me get off him now, so he pulls the material of my pantyhose forward away from my skin and sticks his fingers harshly through until we hear them rip. Now that he has an opening he tears at it, desperate to create an entry for himself. His eyes widen with delight when he sees my bush poking through, glistening with moisture from my arousal.

'No panties Bails?'

'No,' I breathe, happy that he is excited.

'God you're turning me on right now!' His eyes are hungry and wanton, devouring me as they sweep over my entire body. He shoves me back slightly while he unzips his jeans, pulling his pants under his balls to reveal himself to me.

'Come sit on my cock, baby.' His tone is demanding but there is no way I would refuse him. I want him just as much as he wants me. He holds my stockings apart as I lower myself onto him and he lets out a satisfied breath as I sink all the way down his shaft. Rough hands grip my waist and start to rock me back and forth in time to his rhythm.

There is no care or love, just mad insane lust that needs satisfying after the time we have spent apart. Angel pulls me forward, meshing out pelvises together and then pushing me off him again, almost to the point where his cock just about leaves my pussy before shoving himself back deep inside of me. It is a tantalizing tease, bringing me closer and closer to orgasm. I know he is close too. His breathing has quickened and a raspy noise is coming from the back of his throat. Years of being lovers means I know his tells, just as he mine. I am getting too close to the edge.

'Not without me, Bails.' It's a plea that I need to heed.

'No, never without you,' I say, reigning in my desire, switching off the need to come until he is ready with me. A couple more thrusts and I'm going to be completely undone.

'Please, Angel, let me come.'

'Yes, Bailey. Now, come now.' The minute his permission is granted I shatter unashamedly around him. The noises coming out of my throat are guttural and it releases him too. I feel his cock pulsate inside of me, his orgasm reverberating against my most sensitive spots. In the afterglow we are still, holding each other while we get our breath back. As guilty as I should feel, I just don't. I love Angel, would die for him. Knowing that I could never love another more, in this moment I find myself fully committing to moving here to live with him. Everything else I need to sort out – the house, Carron, work – it's all just details.

'Shall we go inside now?' His voice is muffled against my chest.

'Uh-huh.' Gently he slides me off him, all the urgency gone from his movements. Now that we have eradicated the feral need to fuck each other, we can move slowly and take the time to enjoy each other's bodies. I roll off him and slide back into my seat, and laugh loudly at the fogged up windows.

It has begun to grow dark outside in the winter's afternoon, the temperature starting to fall a couple of degrees already. We grab my things and exit the cab, hastening for the front door. It's not locked, as is usual for most folk in the country, and we tumble inside to the glorious warmth that the fireplace has provided. Angel has my bags and toe kicks the front door shut with his boot.

I gaze around at the familiar place, eyes searching for anything that has changed since I've been here last. It's all open-plan and completely made of timber. The smell is heavenly, aged oak filling my senses. On the left is a small kitchen, a wood burning stove already alight and warming a pot of food that sits on top of one of the burners. In the center of the room are a couple of well-worn leather couches that have knit throws over the backs of them. A big fluffy rug covers the floor and there is a bookcase stacked floor to ceiling with novels. Angel loves to read, and has always kept a wide selection of authors on his shelves.

Above this part of the house is a loft which holds Angel's bed. There is a ladder against the wall to access it but my eyes drift to the wall behind the couch. There is a huge oil painting of a naked woman sitting down on the floor, blazing orange hair trailing down her back. The artist has done a magnificent job of recreating the bone structure of the woman. She is lithe and pale, each part of her spine clearly visible to the viewer. Angel can see my gaze lingering.

'It's you. I had a local artist paint it for me.' I half suspected it was me, but still feel gleeful that he has confirmed my suspicions. 'Sort of like having you here, even when you're not,' he says by way of explanation. I'm elated at this bit of information. Kind of because I am and am not gleeful that he is miserable without me. There is a part of me that hates him to be in pain or miserable while we are apart. On the other hand, I am fucking over the moon that he loves me so much that he is suffering when we are not together.

He drops my bags to the floor with a thud, takes my hand and leads me to the bathroom on the far right of the cabin. As is the same with the rest of the privacy of the cabin, there is no door or curtains. The little window affords a wooded view against the dark blue backdrop of evening light. I'm not worried though. There is no one here but us. Angel turns to me and slowly starts to undress me. His touch is caring and lingers whenever his fingers glide across my skin.

Once I'm naked I watch while he removes his own clothes. It is a tortuous striptease that leaves me wanting more. The removal of his clothes leaves nothing but a hard muscled body that ripples when he moves. He reaches across the large claw foot bath tub and turns on the taps. He adds a drop of bath oil and the water starts to froth up as it churns up underneath the water. When the water fills three quarters full, Angel reaches to shut off the taps. Taking my hand he helps me balance as I step into the tub. He climbs in behind me and begins to soap up my body with a sponge.

Every nerve ending is on fire. I'm sure I will never get sick of him touching me. I lean back against his firm chest while his hands go to work on me. My knees jerk in response when his fingers find the middle of my sex. The warm water mixed with the sensation of his touch starts to electrify my body. The ache I feel deep within needs release and Angel knows this by the way I'm writhing under his touch.

His fingers work their magic until I am breathing heavy and panting for it.

'Let me make you come,' he whispers into my ear. There is no encouragement needed. Shortly after, I orgasm beautifully as his fingers rub my clit, stroking me into submission. I'm sated for the time being and as I relax back in his arms I start to feel ravenous. My tummy growls in protest from not having eaten since this morning.

'You're hungry, how rude of me,' he says apologetically.

'Don't be silly. I was hungrier for you first.' He's placated by my remark, but still hurries to get us out of the bath. I'm wrapped in a big fluffy towel while he drips water over the floor. He grabs the spare towel and cinches it around his waist.

'Just a sec, I'll go grab your bag for you.' Angel trots off obediently back into the living room and retrieves the discarded luggage from the floor. He leaves me to get dressed while he goes and gets his own clothes from the cupboard up in the loft. If I was smart I would have hurried after him so I could take full advantage of watching his tight ass climb up the ladder. Instead I hurry to finish dressing and make my way back to the kitchen on the other side of the house.

'Angel?' I shout as I start to rummage through his cupboards.

'Yeah?' His voice echoes up in the loft as it bounces around the high ceiling of the cabin.

'Where are your wine glasses, did you move them?'

'I did. They're on the bottom shelf of the pantry now; I'll be down in just a sec.' Ditching the cupboard I was in I make my way over to the pantry. As promised, the bottom shelf holds the wine glasses I remember us using the last time I was here. On a higher shelf I grab a Cabernet Merlot and take my find to the little table and chairs near the big bay window at the rear of the cabin. There is a candle and matches, so I light it before going to retrieve cutlery for dinner.

'Ah, you found everything I see.' His smile just doesn't get any brighter, his pearly white teeth gleaming at me wolfishly as he goes over to the pot on the stove. The instant the lid is removed the place fills with the wonderful scent of cooked meat in a rich sauce.

'That smells amazing,' I praise, even though I have come to know it's a bit hit and miss with Angel's cooking skills.

'You bet your ass it does.' He ladles two big bowls full and brings it to the table with some bread and organic farm butter. Angel pours our wine while I hungrily tuck into the lamb shanks. Compared to Carron's culinary skills, Angel's pale in comparison. The food is definitely edible, but it lacks the layers that a more seasoned cook would add to the meal. We don't talk, the wine and food occupying us for the time being. When I can eat no more, I sit back full and content.

'Want to stay up and read for a while?' he asks me.

'I know it's really early still, but can we go snuggle in bed?'

'You're asking me if we can snuggle in bed? Are you kidding me?'

'I guess that's a yes then?'

'Consider that a fucking hell yes.'

Eighteen

Morning comes in the blink of an eye. It's Saturday and I realize as I am coming back into the land of the living that I completely forgot to call or text Carron last night to tell him I made it safely to Chicago. Not that I am in Chicago, but Carron is none the wiser. I groan as I struggle to open my eyes. Angel comes into focus next to me. He is lying still on his side, already awake and dark eyes watching me intently.

'Morning.' His voice is husky, tickling my nerve endings.

'Hey.'

'You want coffee?'

'Please.' Not that I want to be rid of Angel, but I know he will not be impressed if I pick up the phone and start calling Carron in front of him. I watch as Angel takes off down the ladder and scramble for my handbag he put next to my side of the bed last night. The minute I slide the lock screen off my phone I curse that I was so stupid. There are five text messages and just as many missed calls, all from Carron of course. Pressing the redial button I anxiously wait while the call is connected.

'Bailey?'

'Hi, Carron,' I muster in as quiet as voice as possible.

'Are you all right, Bailey? I've been really worried about you, especially seems I haven't heard from you all night.' I'm a horrible, horrible person, but it does not stop the untruths from spilling from my mouth. I sit up on the bed, ready to spew forth some spectacular excuse.

'I'm so sorry, Carron. It's stupid really. My cell fell out of my pocket in the cab on the way to the hotel. It took forever to get back as the driver didn't head back to the company until late in the evening.'

'You could have called from the hotel.' I'm ashamed that I have caused him so much anguish and promise myself that I will end it with him the minute I get back. This isn't becoming fair on anyone.

'I know, and I'm sorry. My meetings went over time and by the time I got back to my room I just needed to crash. Let me make it up to you when I get back, okay?'

'Sure, Bails. Just remember that I love you like crazy, okay?'

'I'll remember, Carron. I really am sorry to worry you. When I get back tomorrow night how about we go out for dinner?'

'That would be great – I've got the night off too.' Carron's tone has brightened at my suggestion, but I still can't help feeling like the biggest snake ever.

'Great. Well I have to go; I have a client waiting for me.'

'Okay, Bailey. Love you, honey.'

'I'll send you a text message when I board my flight tomorrow, all right?'

'Sounds great. Bye, honey.'

'Bye.' He doesn't say anything about me ending the conversation without an 'I love you'. While I sit on the edge of the bed for a second, I wonder why he's never said anything about that. Pushing the thought to the back of my mind I decide to get dressed and join Angel downstairs. Hopping off the bed I stand and spin around and notice he is standing at the top of the ladder, coffee cup in hand. His face is dark as thunder and he does not look impressed at all.

'Hey, I didn't see you there.' I allow a little smile, hoping to lessen the hurt he must be feeling.

'Obviously. What the hell are you doing talking to *him* while you're here with me? I thought you were leaving him, isn't that why you're here?' His words are scathing, like a hot poker on my skin.

'Of course I am,' I plead, 'but I can't just ditch him overnight, Angel, that wouldn't be fair.'

'Who, to him or me?' Oh, he's more than just a little mad and it makes the tears prick at the corner of my eyes.

'I don't want to hurt either of you, but of course I want to be with you. I always have, Angel. Just remember you're the one who pushed me away in the first place because you said that we were living in sin!' I'm struggling to catch my breath, rage pouring over me in huge waves.

'Bails, I…'

'No! You, listen to me, Angel. Not once have I ever rejected you or pushed you away. Never! It has only ever been you. But when you called it off and practically pushed me into someone else's arms just to make yourself feel better about the whole situation I did what I thought you wanted me to do.' My exasperation is bleeding out of me and draining my resolve to be angry at him.

'I never wanted you to be with someone else,' he says somberly.

'Then why in fuck did you tell me to do it! Don't you know I have only ever done everything I can to try and please you, damn it?'

'I know and I'm sorry. What I asked of you was unfair on you and to be honest it has done nothing but torture me. At the time I thought it was the right thing to do for both of us. I thought if you were with someone else, you'd forget about me. And I thought if I saw you were happy then I could finally leave you alone.'

'Didn't quite work out like that though, did it?' I spit.

'No.' He's mollified for the minute.

'God, Angel. You could have saved us both a lot of heartache if you'd just given into us a long time ago.'

'I know. I'm sorry, okay?' The look on his face softens me instantly. I dry my eyes and relent on the anger that burst out of me moments ago.

'Me too,' I sigh. Angel climbs the last few stairs and approaches me cautiously. He extends the coffee mug out towards me as a peace offering.

'Forgiven?'

'I'll think about it.' The look on my face is smug, but he knows I'm joking. I take the mug he proffers to me and take a big gulp. It's warm and milky and hits the spot. He watches intently while I drink it, my gaze holding his.

'Can I ask you something?'

'Sure,' I reply.

'You're gonna move here, right?'

'You bet. And I'm not going to let you ever get rid of me this time, despite how wrong you think our relationship is.'

'Shit, Bails. I may think our relationship is wrong, but I know you are absolutely perfect for me. There isn't a single woman on this earth who holds my eye the way you do.' If my soul could sing right now, I'm sure it would.

'Well good, because I think you're a bit of okay yourself.' Snatching the mug out of my hand he puts it on the side drawer before throwing me back onto the bed. He straddles my waist and pins my arms up behind my head.

'So, you're going to tell him it's over right?'

'Yes, I promise.'

'And you're going to move back here with me, right?'

'Yes.'

'And you're going to let me make love to you for the rest of your life, right?'

'I could think of worse things,' I tease. He bites his lip at my last remark and his eyes close just a little as he pretends to glare at me.

'You better let me, or I might just have to force you.' His tone is lighthearted, but I know he's a tiny bit serious.

'You know I would never deny you access to my body.'

'I know. That was the biggest mistake you ever made.' His expression turns sad and I instantly regret my choice of words.

'Don't say that, Angel. I love you, all of you, and there will never be a single moment in my entire life that I will ever regret letting you touch me – not ever, do you hear me?' He nods and bends to kiss me deeply. I don't know if I have him fully convinced, but at least in my opinion we are a step in the right direction. Now all I have to figure out is how to tell Carron that things between us are over.

Nineteen

After breakfast we head on over to Angel's stables where he keeps his stock of Clydesdales. They're often needed around the mill to pull logs or equipment when some of the mechanical alternatives are faulty. In their down time, Angel rides them over his property and along the bordering national park. He saddles them quickly, his deft hands moving over the leather and buckles. I watch, fascinated that he is such a capable human being, but remind myself this is why I fell in love with him in the first place.

He takes both horses by the reins and leads them to the stable door. The snow has stopped for the minute, but clouds continue to roll endlessly across the sky. We both have jackets and boots on to protect us from the cold, but the nip in the air still bites at my cheeks. I get a leg up from Angel and straddle the horse, knees gripping its girth for stability. There is no assistance for him; he doesn't need it. Strong arms with muscles made from being a physical laborer allow him to pull himself into the saddle in one fell swoop.

'Why, sir, I do believe you've done that before.' My southern accent brings a smile to his lips and I love the way his eyes crinkle in the corners as his whole face comes alive.

'Ma'am, you may just be right about that.' He tips is hat to me and then uses his heels to kick his horse to move forward. Fuck a man in uniform; I'd take a cowboy over them any day. I trot after him on my horse as he picks out a trail that leads away from the house. We are both good riders, although because he does it all the time he is a little more comfortable in the saddle. I keep up with his cantering pace, though, and we fly through the woods with exhilaration. We pass a stream where we let the horses drink. I notice Angel is staring at me weirdly. Well, weirdly for him anyway.

'What?'

'I was just thinking…'

'Yeah?'

'There's a little coffee house not far from here on the outskirts of the national park. They've got a big log fire and the best hot chocolate. Anyway, I was thinking… maybe we could go for a drink?' I'm speechless. Never have we allowed ourselves to be seen together in a public setting like he is suggesting. Our love affair has always been very guarded. I guess if I moved here to be with Angel then we wouldn't have to worry about being that way anymore.

'You mean like a date?'

'Yes, our first date.' His face erupts into a full blown grin. 'What do you reckon?'

'Yes, I'd like that very much.' His enthusiasm is spreading over me and a thrill of excitement storms my chest. He takes his reins in his hands and pulls his horse's head in the direction he wants to go. Angel's expression is playful and cheeky as his eyes sweep over me.

'Think you can keep up?'

'You bet your ass I can.' I grab my reins too and follow after him at a gallop. Adrenalin spikes through my blood as I chase him through the woods. The speed we are going is insane. I could fall off for God's sake! But I am having too much fun to care for my safety. My horse's spit froths around the bit as it gives chase. My mood is that electric and free that I feel like laughing at the top of my lungs. I clench my mouth shut and ignore the sting of the wind as it burns my cheeks. We play a game of chase as we thunder across the snowy ground and I'm quite disappointed when a clearing comes into view. I pull up on the reins and my horse obliges by slowing its pace. Angel also pulls up his steed and turns to wait for me to reach him.

The pink glow on my cheeks does not go unnoticed by him.

'Having fun?'

'Lots,' I say.

'Your cheeks are all flushed.'

'I feel great. Free as a bird.'

'Come on, let's get out of the cold.' We ride on a bit further from the main road and come to stop outside a chalet-style cabin. Plumes of smoke fan out of the chimney top and linger on the light wind that trails the valley. The smell of pine needles linger. Outside of the coffee house are a couple of cars and a motorcycle. We add our horses to the mix and trudge up the steps to enter.

Inside is warm and inviting. A massive stone fireplace dominates the center of the house and comfy booths surround it. We take up position in one further away from the other patrons and wait for the waitress to serve us. I sit next to Angel, but keep my distance as is habit when we go out in public together. He reaches out for the belt loop in the back of my jeans and drags my ass across the cushioned seat so that I am sitting comfortably in the crook of his arm and leaning against his muscled body. My heart falters and I pray to God I won't pass out right here.

He leans in close and whispers in my ear. 'You don't need to shy away from me here, no one knows us, remember?'

'It's a hard habit to break,' I whisper back.

'Well you better get over it because I'm not going to keep my paws off you now that I have you here.' I smile, delighted at his possessiveness over me. An older lady with a kindly face approaches our table with a pen and pad in hand.

'Hello, folks, is there something I can get for you?'

'Yes please. We'll have two hot chocolates with marshmallows, white ones please.' Angel knows I can't stand the pink ones.

'Sure thing. Would you like lunch too?'

'I think we'll grab some soup – what do you have today?'

'It's homemade minestrone.'

'That will do nicely, thank you.' He smiles at her as she walks off to place our order with the kitchen. I'm happy we came, and snuggle as close to Angel as I can get without actually sitting on his lap. He buries his face in my hair and trails kisses up the side of my neck which gives me goose bumps up my arms, despite the sweater and jacket I'm wearing.

'Damn you smell good, makes me want to eat you.'

'Maybe you can eat me later,' I say suggestively, raising one eyebrow up as I do.

'You're a tease, you know that?'

'Mmm.' It's all I can muster as he starts to nibble on my ear lobe. I'm suddenly wishing that we were in a more private place. The waitress comes back with our drinks and soup and we tuck heartily in, momentarily forgetting our other needs. We are relaxed and comfortable. So much so that the afternoon passes and we are still snuggled in the booth and decide to share a bottle of wine. The Merlot is a European import and slides smoothly down my throat. There is no aftertaste, just a rich body of fruity notes with a hint of oak that work well in relaxing my body. We chat and giggle like teenagers, finally getting to relish the behavior I skipped at that age.

'Better go before more snow descends upon us,' he says.

'I'm already feeling stiff; I don't think I can move.'

'You better, Bails, or you'll be stuck here for the night.'

'Okay, but I'm stealing a warm bath when we get back.'

'Deal. I'll even soap your back for you.'

'Now that is something I cannot say no to.' I shuffle out of the booth followed closely by Angel. He leaves money on the table for the bill and adds a little extra for the tip. We thank the waitress on the way out and promise to visit again soon. Angel gives me a leg up again onto my horse, although it seems more difficult than this morning. I am pleasantly numb and tell Angel we should go a little slower on the way back. My reaction time is not as quick and that is entirely to do with the fact I have consumed too much wine.

We head off riding side by side, just as the first of the snowflakes start to float down from the sky. Even though it takes us longer to get back to his cabin, time seems to fly by quickly. I'm blissfully happy and do not notice the abundance of snowflakes that has already fallen around us.

'We better hope we don't get snowed in tonight.' I look at him in alarm.

'You don't really think we would do you?' Panic momentarily seizes me.

'We should be okay. The weather report did mention we were expecting an unusual amount of snowfall this weekend, but nothing a shovel and snow chains can't fix.' I heave a sigh of relief.

'Won't do if my flight is cancelled, I need to get back tomorrow.'

'I know you do.' The dark mood resurfaces on his face. He's never been great with goodbyes. We arrive back at the stables and give the horses a quick brush down and settle them back in their stalls with fresh hay and water. Angel locks up the barn door and takes my hand as we head to the house.

'Why don't you go have a soak while I get dinner on?' he offers.

'Don't you want to join me?'

'Don't fucking tempt me. But with all that riding and alcohol you've just had I'm sure you're going to need a meal real soon. So go ahead, I'll take advantage of you later.'

Happy Angel is back. I like him much better.

I retreat to the bathtub and draw the water as hot as I can stand it. Once in I allow myself to sink in all the way up to my chin. My hair is piled up in a messy bun on my head and it acts as a pillow as I lean back against the porcelain and close my eyes. As my body relaxes, I drift off into a peaceful sleep.

We have just made love. It was wonderful. He made my body tremble with pleasure as his tongue lapped at the lips of my sex, bringing me closer to orgasm. His hands fumbled all over my body, not knowing what to touch next without fully having indulged in the last bit of flesh that took his attention. He wouldn't let me come with his mouth though. Instead he fills me with his cock and urges me along slowly as we ride the wave of euphoria. He seems skilled in the art of lovemaking, but my possessive side dares not ask how he knows how to do the things he does to me. Just the thought of him being with another woman makes me sick with jealousy. Instead I concentrate on how much I love him, and he me. My mind fills with how good this feels.

We both climax together and my body quivers in delight. I know that I am ruined for another. I will never get sick of being with him like this. Our post glow sex is ruined by a voice that floats down the hallway towards me. It is my mother.

'Bailey? Are you in your room honey?'

'Fuck!' Angel curses and I mimic his reaction to a tee. We both agree that there is no way in hell she can find us in here together. We would never live it down. Angel scrambles to put his clothes on and lifts the window to my room. He jumps out onto the ledge and hisses that he will see me later. All I have time for is a shirt and pull the duvet up over my lower body to cover my nakedness.

The door flings open and my mother walks in.

'Bailey! What are you doing in bed this early in the afternoon?' She takes in my flushed cheeks and perspiration on my forehead. 'Aren't you well, dear?'

'Not really,' I lie. 'I think I'm coming down with something.' Yeah, it's called lyingitis.

'Oh that's no good, honey. Well stay in bed, won't you and I'll bring you supper later, okay?'

'Sure, Mom.' She closes the door to my bedroom and I flop back against my pillow. That… was too damn close. From now on we were going to have to be more careful. There was no way I was going to let Angel in my room again after that. That's when we started having sex in his car every night. That way we were assured our privacy.

'Bailey?' The water around me has gone tepid and I realize that I must have dozed off in the tub.

'Yeah?' I yawn loudly and hurry to get out of the water.

'Dinner's ready!' Angel is yelling from the kitchen. I fling a robe around me and pad across the floor boards in his direction. He has the fire going nicely and the cabin is toasty as I join him at the table.

'You were ages.'

'Sorry, I fell asleep.' He snickers at me as he serves chicken and pasta onto my plate.

'Typical girl.'

'Hey,' I complain, taking a swipe at his ass while he walks around me. He jumps out the way, but I glare at him in indignation instead.

'No hitting the help,' he chastises as he puts the tea towel over his arm and pretends to act the role of butler.

'Wine, ma'am?'

'No thank you, sir. I feel your intentions are not honorable and you just want to get in my panties.'

'I always want to get in your panties, regardless of whether you've had a drink or not.'

'Well in that case, kind sir, please pour me a small glass to accompany this mouthwatering meal you have served me.' He obliges and then joins me at the table. The pasta is seasoned with herbs and lemon zest, while fresh spinach, tomatoes and feta accompany the chicken. It's delicious and I eat twice as much as I normally would for dinner.

'God, Bails, if you keep eating like that you'll eat me out of house and home.'

'Must be the mountain air and all the sex we're having. So if you want me to eat less you're going to have to stop fucking me.'

'That'll never happen,' he deadpans. I smile sweetly at him but continue with my meal. Afterwards we retire to the leather sofa and he wraps us up in a blanket. He's selected Moby Dick off the bookshelf and proceeds to read to me – stroking my hair while I hug his chest. Outside the snow storm rages and rattles the window frames of the cabin. We both end up falling asleep here, the book falling to the floor unnoticed as we drift away to the land of nod.

Twenty

Morning brings relief that the storm wasn't as bad as the weather reports had previously predicted, although I think Angel secretly wished we had been snowed in so as to delay my departure. I remind him that the quicker I leave to sort things back out in Astoria, the quicker I can return to him. He doesn't look convinced.

We share a strained breakfast of pancakes and coffee before I head upstairs to pack my few bits and pieces into my carry on suitcase.

'So what are you going to do about the house?'

I think for a minute before replying.

'I love that house and really don't want to sell it. At the same time, Carron needs somewhere to live. I think the best scenario is if he just stays there and pays rent into the mortgage account for the time being.'

'And you think he's just going to readily accept you walking away?'

'He'll have to,' I say firmly.

'What about work?'

'I'll contact Maria as soon as I'm back and ask her if I can work out of office. As you said, I do most of my stuff via internet or interstate when working on a project, so I can't see it would be a problem. They have other members of staff who work from home because their location doesn't permit them working from an office either.'

'So how soon will you be back?'

'Maybe a couple of weeks.'

'A couple of weeks! Shit, Bails, I really don't want to wait that long. Can't you get here any faster?'

'I'm not sure. There are things I want to bring with me, but I won't be able to fit all that in my car, so I guess I will have to see when a movers can swing by and pick up the pieces I want to bring.'

'I'll give you two weeks max, Bails. I don't want to wait any longer than that. The thought of you still being in the same house as him makes me cringe.'

'He's a good man, Angel, and he's done nothing but support and love me despite the fact I have been nothing but an unreceptive bitch since we got together,' I snap. Angel is silenced momentarily. He knows I am right, but it doesn't mean he has to like it one bit.

'Two weeks. How about I drive down with one of the work trucks and I can bring your stuff back for you. That way you don't have to wait for the movers and I can drive behind you on the way back here.' I can't help but smile. He really is trying hard to pull out all the stops to get me back here quicker.

'Okay, but promise me one thing.'

'Anything.'

'Don't say another mean word about Carron. I mean it, Angel, he deserves better than the likes of us being anywhere near him.' He can see I mean business, so he relents.

'Fine. Doctor Boy is off my shit list, anything else?'

'Yes. You can come over here and fuck my pussy so I will still remember what it feels like in two weeks when you come to get me.'

Angel's eyes light up like a Christmas tree.

'Now *that* I can do,' he growls as he lunges for me. He pins me down on the bed and nudges my legs apart with his knees. His mouth is hot and feverish as it finds my own and his tongue commands me to tangle with his. I pry my hands out from under his grip and fist his hair in them. He moans quietly on top of me and continues to maul me. His eyes are lustful when he finally breaks away and they take in the shirt that covers my chest. Without hesitation he grabs the middle where the buttons hold it together and rips it roughly so that they pop off and sound against the wooden floor.

I gasp with delight as his hands yank my bra down to reveal my breasts. His mouth savors each nipple, sucking hard until they are pink buds standing to attention on my chest. He trails his tongue down the flat of my belly and nips me hard when his momentum is interrupted by my pants.

Angel pushes off me and fumbles with the button and then yanks them crudely off my ankles. My panties are met with the same disrespect that my shirt was and he rips the thin material off my bottom without any hesitation. He throws the material onto his bedside table.

'You're not getting those back,' he whispers huskily. 'They're mine to remember you while you're gone.' *Hot, very hot*. I can just imagine him taking delight in sniffing my panties. Fuck. I'm so wet and my juices are flowing out of me, preparing me for what is to come. Angel doesn't bother to undress. He manages to slide his shirt off, but that's about it.

He pulls his cock out the top of his tracksuit pants and then lies back down on top of me, his warm flesh meeting my own.

I close my eyes, succumbing to the delight.

'Open your eyes; I want to look into your soul as I enter you.' His plea is desperate. He cannot hold back any longer. My eyelids flicker open and I gasp when he immediately thrusts himself inside of me. He presses deeply, filling me with him in his entirety.

'Oh, Bailey, I love you so much, baby. Don't ever go.' I kiss his lips as he moves inside of me, quashing his fears that I would ever leave him. We move slowly, rhythmically. Ours is a dance that only connected souls will ever feel. When a relationship is devoid of this, you certainly know it. This man above me is mine, and I am his. There will only ever be the two of us – loving until the end of time.

Our tempo increases, frantic almost. The desire has peaked and we are balancing on the edge. I think he is going to bring us home when he grabs underneath my ass and pulls me with him as he stands up. He moves to the windowsill where he sits my ass on the ledge, the flesh of my cheeks pressing hard against the cold glass. Pounding into me his breathing becomes more erratic.

'Come with me,' he demands. I grab his buttocks and pull him deeper and harder. He grinds against my clit as he pushes back and forth. I'm so close. Climaxing loudly sends Angel into wave of pleasure. I reach behind his thigh to stroke his balls as he comes. We calm as we come down from the crescendo. Being here with Angel is definitely the right move. This way we can be together without another single soul knowing who we really are.

Twenty-One

The flight back to Astoria is a miserable one. I hide under the complimentary blanket the airline provides and pretend I am on my own. Leaving Angel is bad enough for sure, but it is the impending heartache I am about to inflict that has me in distress. I wish I had just been a big girl and stayed on my own. But in a way, I thought I was pleasing Angel by moving on with Carron.

When I first met Carron, Angel was going through all kinds of crises about the morality of our relationship. He had come to Astoria unannounced one day and saw Carron and I getting coffee together. We were just friends then, getting our caffeine fixes after my arm had been set in cast. We didn't even plan to meet, we just ran into each other in the coffee shop. Angel happened to drive by and see us. After that he told me we couldn't see each other anymore and I should be happy and move on 'with that guy I saw you with', because at least then I could go out in public and enjoy the relationship. To be honest, I think we both regret that things went that way.

The wheels of the plane touch down and I cringe internally. He's going to be waiting on the other side of the departure door, excited and ready to take me out to dinner. I'm not wrong.

He runs towards me, thrilled at the sight of me. I try to muster some excitement but only come up with a watery smile.

'Hey, Bailey, I've missed you.' He grabs me in a bear hug; squishing my insides and making me feel even more queasy than I already did.

'Hey, Carron.' My voice is muffled against his jacket and I struggle to release myself from his grip.

'So, how was your trip huh?' His smile dims somewhat when he finally takes in my mood and expression.

'Not the best. Things were a bit hectic work-wise and you know, all that drama with losing my phone and what not…' The lies just seem to pour out of me. I really don't know where they come from.

'Oh, you poor thing! I completely forgot about the shitty start to your trip. Don't worry now, you're back home safe and I'm going to spoil you and take you out for dinner.'

'Thanks, Carron. That sounds… nice.' Carron isn't really listening. His jovial mood is firmly in place as he grabs my bag and heads towards the exit doors. I trail after him, wondering just how I am going to work up the courage to tell him we're over. *You could start by stopping the lies. Right, like that's ever going to happen.*

The drive over to the restaurant is filled with his chatter about his weekend. There was the fishing trip, work, beers with Eddy and a hike up over the cliff tops with a group from his work.

'Sounds like you've been busy,' I offer. He glances sideways at me while he's driving. I know what he's thinking straight away and wish I had just kept my big mouth shut and stuck to the non-committal reply I had offered previously.

'Don't get me wrong, Bailey. I missed you terribly, even though I had a lot to do.' He places his hand over mine and resumes his conversation. Always looking out for my feelings is just Carron's way.

We pull up outside a swank restaurant down near the old wharf. The décor is all crystal and white walls and I begin to wonder what the special occasion is. I take in Carron's attire and I'm beginning to think I am underdressed in my plain wool knit and long black skirt with boots. Removing my hairband from the bun on top of my head, I shake my hair loose so that I might appear a little more sophisticated. The waiter greets us at the door and offers to take our jackets before seating us at a table for four.

'What are we doing here?' I hiss while the waiter pours us water and hands us our menu. I begrudgingly get out a thank you to the waiter before turning my attention back to getting an answer out of Carron. He continues with his annoying smile and offers no explanation. Knowing I should just put him out of his misery as soon as possible, I decide that I should just get this over with and tell him our relationship is over now.

Too late. Mr. Annoying Waiter is back at our table with people accompanying him. I peer past him rudely to take in the couple. They are older, probably early sixties. Sophisticated and impeccably dressed. The woman looks like she has shares in Laura Ashley and the man holds himself with importance. Well of course he should. It hits me now. I've met them before at a hospital function. The man is Dr.

Simon Simons. I remember the name because at the time I thought it utterly absurd that a parent would actually be stupid enough to name their child with the same first and last name.

Carron jumps up to greet them and offers them the empty chairs at our table.

'Bailey honey, you remember Doctor Simons and his wife Julia from the charity ball last year don't you?'

'Of course.' I stand to shake their hands and plaster a very fake smile on my lips. 'How have you both been?' My tone is polite but forced.

'Very well, my dear!' Doctor Simons' voice booms across the table at me and I feel like I have just been slapped in the face from the force of it. Shit, if he were my husband I would soon be deaf from the ear trauma caused. 'Even better now that I am retiring,' he adds with a wink.

'Oh, congratulations,' I offer. His wife is smiling like a Cheshire cat and Carron has the stupid grin happening too. What is with these people? I'm beginning to wonder if they've all been drinking the same happy juice.

'Well it's not me I think you should be congratulating, m'dear!' Boom, boom. 'Your fiancé is in the lucky position of taking over my role as chief of staff at the hospital in the emergency department.' He claps his hands in delight and the effect is just as supersonic as his voice. *Oh fucking shit.* This little bit of news puts a real spanner in my works. There is no way I can break up with Carron tonight. I'd be totally killing his career buzz and end up looking like the biggest shitheel that ever graced the face of this earth. Fuck, fuck, fucketty fuck.

So I swallow my plans to abort this relationship, slap a huge smile on my own face and offer Carron my congratulations.

The only thing I can hope for now is that they all get that stinking drunk while celebrating Carron's success that he won't be in any state to pester me for sex when we get home later.

Twenty-Two

To: bails@quickmail.com
From: thurmontlumberyard@wizzmail.net
Subject: My heart is in your hands
No word from you. It's been a few days since your return to Astoria. What happened? Did you tell him? Not about us of course, but that you're leaving. I'm getting impatient. My heart is hurting…
I need you.
Angel.

To: thurmontlumberyard@wizzmail.net
From: bails@quickmail.com
Subject: Worry wart…
I'm yours, and I always will be. Disaster the first night back in town. Dinner organized at restaurant – was going to tell him there, I swear. Unexpected events… he got a promotion and invited his predecessor. There was no way to ruin the evening. I will tell him I promise. Patience. I will wait for you… on the porch on the 14th February. Kind of fitting, don't you think? Valentine's Day. The day I really get to have your heart for the rest of my life.
Yours,
Bails xx

To: *bails@quickmail.com*
From: *thurmontlumberyard@wizzmail.net*
Subject: *Forever*

Music to my ears – you being mine forever. I'm never going to let you go. Not ever. Listening to Mumford & Sons 'I will wait' on repeat. Counting the days, hours, minutes, seconds until I lay eyes on you again. Truck is ready. Expect me – there is nothing on this earth that is going to keep me from you. Nothing.

Angel.

To: *thurmontlumberyard@wizzmail.net*
From: *bails@quickmail.com*
Subject: *Everything that I am...*

I lay down at your feet. My heart, my soul, my love for you are yours to keep for the rest of our lives. You're right – there is nothing that will keep you from me this time. I won't allow it. Patiently waiting,

Bails xx

I sign off the email and press send. It's a quiet day at the office and all my scheduled work is complete. Only four days have passed since returning from Thurmont but I have already started to weave my web of plans to make my hasty exit. To be honest, at this stage I'm not even sure I will tell Carron. I think I lack the guts to say it to his face and at this stage I'm thinking I might take the coward's way out and leave him a note, one that is descriptive and detailed in my reasoning for leaving him. A list of arrangements so far as the house is concerned will also have to be included. Still, I think I will decide last minute which is the best approach to take.

Maria has already received my letter to ask for a transfer from the office to work via internet on assignment in Thurmont rather than being stationed in Astoria. Her return email popped up in my inbox with a resonate ping. Consumed with nervous tension I let my mouse hover over the open button while I calm myself. One click. That's all that was needed to bring the biggest smile to my face.

My eyes scan the letter quickly, seeking out the most important bits and digesting what the information means.

... application has been approved... accept your proposal for employment via internet... your new location of Thurmont, Maryland.

I restrain myself from jumping out of my seat and squealing in delight. I want to email Angel and tell him the good news, but I know it won't matter either way. He's coming for me whether I get a job transfer or not. I'm sitting in my chair, smug with a grin as wide as the Amazon plastered on my face. Lyra walks into the office and stops abruptly when she sees me.

'Why the hell are you grinning like that?'

'Ah, no reason.' I try to wipe the smile from my face, but to be honest the task is next to impossible right now.

'Right, that's it! Grab your coat. You and I are going for lunch and you are going to tell me what's going on with you right now, young lady!' Lyra is not about to take no for answer. I think my best course of action here is to just tell her as much of the truth as I can without divulging

169

everything. Otherwise she's going to be like a dog with a bone and not relent until she gets some answers.

'Okay, but let's make it a quick one – I still have stuff to email off to Maria before the publishing cut off this afternoon.'

'Fine by me. Move your ass girl! It's time you spilled your guts!'

We head down the street to a café that isn't frequented by the regulars in the area. Their food is priced higher than our normal haunt and not nearly as nice. We decide we need the privacy, though, and enter the deserted shop. Lyra places our order at the counter and then joins me at a table in the corner of the store, out of the view of the foot traffic walking by on the sidewalk. She unwraps her scarf from around her neck and removes her jacket, carefully placing it over the back of her chair. She takes her seat and then sets me squarely with her gaze.

'What's going on with you?'

'What makes you think anything is going on?'

'Don't bullshit a bullshitter, Bailey. We've been friends for a long time, and despite the fact I normally spill my guts to you about my personal problems, I am not without an emotion detector. Now you normally keep your private stuff to yourself, which is cool, but this time I can feel something big is going on. Your mood is up and down and you're distracted. So spill.'

'Okay. I'll tell you, but only if your promise not to tell a soul. Ever. No matter how much someone might try and torture the truth out of you, you can never spill your guts.'

'Oooh, this sounds so melodramatic! Go ahead, Bails, I'm all ears.' She leans forward perceptibly to get closer to me.

'I mean it. This stays between you and me.' She uses her finger to make a cross over her chest.

'Swear,' she promises.

'Well, I'm leaving Astoria.'

'What? With Carron?'

'No.'

'On your own? You mean he's not going with you?'

'Yes, and no he is not coming with me.'

'Let me get this straight. You're leaving Astoria, where you have a house and a fiancé, not to mention your job, why?'

'Because I'm in love with someone else.' Her mouth hangs open, agape with shock.

'What the fuck, Bailey? I'm taking it Carron knows nothing about this someone else?'

'No he doesn't.'

'Well the decent thing would be to tell him, you know. And who is this other guy? You've never once mentioned you're having an affair.'

'I'll tell Carron in my own time. Trust me, I know he deserves to know now, but the right time just hasn't come up yet.'

'So when do you plan on leaving?'

'Ten days.'

'Ten days!' Lyra's screeching voice resonates off the walls of the café, just as our meals arrive at the table. I take a swipe at her arm.

'Be quiet,' I hiss.

'Well, sor-ry! Fucking hell, Bailey. Ten days? How long have you been planning this? Don't you think it would have been fair to let everyone in on it?'

'Look I'm not proud of the fact that people are going to get hurt here. The truth is, I just can't keep living a lie anymore. I love Carron, really I do. But I'm not in love with him. My heart has never been with him. We've made some wonderful memories but being in love with someone else means that I could never fully give myself to him and allow our relationship to go further.'

'I see.' She's hurt that I haven't confided in her sooner and her body language says as much.

'Lyra, I never meant to hurt you either. I just don't talk about my personal shit – with anyone. There's things about my past that I can never share with anyone, because if I open even one little floodgate, I'm afraid all my secrets are going to unravel.' She looks at me confused.

'What secrets?'

'It doesn't matter. None of it does anymore. But something's happened and I have the chance to finally live my life the way I want to, with whom I want to.'

'So, you're just going to give up everything you have worked so hard for here?'

'To me the sacrifice is worth it.' She looks sad, maybe even disappointed.

'Will you stay in touch? Or come back to visit?'

'I'll stay in touch with you for sure,' I promise. 'I'll still be working for Danzar, just via email and on the net, rather than from the office here in Astoria.' She seems slightly placated at this bit of news.

'So we may even run into each other on assignments?'

'That's right, we could – we've always been a good team you and I.'

'What about coming back here to visit? And your house?'

'I'm going to offer Carron to stay there for the time being. I don't think I will be back for a while... let the dust settle and all that.' She's taking everything in, obviously hurt by my deception as well. I realize now that more people will be hurt by this than I first thought. The thing is, I would do it all again to be given the opportunity to be with Angel. I decide I must be a cold-hearted, callous bitch to be so unfeeling. I think I have felt so much love for Angel that maybe I didn't have room left for anyone else.

'Well you know I would love to keep in touch with you, right?'

'Of course! I'm going to make sure Maria gives us the same assignments from time to time just so we can catch up and do the whole girly get-together thing you love so much.' She smiles gratefully at me.

'I'd like that.' *Please don't cry*, I silently beg. I hate other people's tears. I think that is half the reason why I haven't been able to face Carron yet – I don't think I'm strong enough to bear seeing him cry.

'Well good, 'cause you can't get rid of me that easily.'

'You're going to tell Carron though, aren't you?'

'Yes,' I reply hesitantly.

'Bailey...'

'I know, I know. I will, but I don't just want to spring it on him. Don't you say a word to him though, you promised remember.' Panic suddenly fills me. Would Lyra's moral compass force her to betray our friendship so she can tell Carron the truth about my intentions? She is thoughtful, but nods her head.

'I won't tell him, Bailey. That's not my place.' I let out a sigh of relief.

'Thank you, Lyra, I appreciate it.' We attempt to make small talk as we finish up our lunch, although the conversation is strained. We've been friends for many years, but like all of my relationships, nobody ever really gets to know the real me.

We finish up and head back to the office. Lyra disappears, claiming she has work to do at home. The rest of the gang are interstate at the moment, so I am left alone to see out the work day. I spend the rest of my day organizing my banking and contact details for the move to Maryland.

Carron has been working non-stop since he was given his promotion. We haven't really had a spare minute to catch up at all since I have been back, but I know Lyra is right about telling him the truth. I owe him that much. Once I've settled on a plan to cook him dinner before telling him the truth, I call him at work to arrange it. He answers his cell on the fourth ring.

'Hello?' He sounds harassed, which is not like him at all.

'Hi, Carron, sorry is this a bad time?'

'No, honey, you're fine. I'm just running up to the lab to get some results for a patient I'm treating in the ER. What's up?'

'I was just wondering if you'd be home for dinner tonight.' There is a rustle of papers and a pause as he notes the time on his watch.

'Ah, it's almost 5:00 now – would you mind holding off until 7:00?'

'Sure, I'll have dinner ready for when you get home.' Nervousness works its way to the pit of my belly.

'Thanks, Bails, you're the best. See you soon.'

'Bye.' I place the receiver back in its place and pray I have the strength to go through with it.

Twenty-Three

I make Carron's favorite meal – beef stroganoff with white fluffy rice. Somehow, I think the act of kindness will soften the blow of the news I am about to dump on him. Jezebel gets underfoot as I cook on the stove, and I realize my nights of cooking in this kitchen are limited. Over the coming days I'm going to have to start putting the stuff I want to take with me into boxes so that when Angel comes I will have everything in the one place.

Ditching the dining table, I set two places on the coffee table in the living room. My intention is to make Carron as comfortable as possible. Not that it will make any difference to his reaction, but I think an informal setting is more appropriate tonight. I open a bottle of wine and leave it to breathe while I fetch a couple of glasses from the kitchen. Deciding I need a stiff drink for courage, I go to the liquor cabinet and fetch out Carron's best scotch. A couple of healthy swigs later and I feel the buzz flow through my body. I can do this, I tell myself.

Carron shouldn't be too far away, so I sit in the front window seat, watching the driveway for the headlights of his car. I'm like a child waiting for the man of the house to come back home. Only this reunion will not be a happy one.

Through the sheer curtains I can see his car coming up the driveway, momentarily blinding me. I hurry to the back door, eager to meet Carron as he comes in. It is important I set the mood for the evening. Just as I swing open the door he is trotting up the steps to come in.

'Bails! Hey, baby.' He doesn't wait for me to say anything. He breezes in through the door and takes me in his arms, planting a huge peck on my cheek. That's definitely not what I had in mind.

'Hey, Carron. How was work?'

'Busy. I've been there since six o'clock this morning. Oh my God, is that beef stroganoff I can smell?'

'Ah, yeah.' My voice sounds weak even to my own ears. He seems not to notice though.

'You're the best, you know that?' He slaps me on the ass and takes off in the direction of the stairs. 'I'm just gonna grab a shower before we eat, okay?' He doesn't wait for a response as he heads up the stairs. I hear the shower go on and him singing loudly to himself. He's happy. Fuck, and I'm going to ruin it big time.

I turn on the television and wait for him to join me. It's good background noise, but I'm not paying any attention to the stories. My head continually runs over how to broach the conversation with him. I think being straightforward is going to be my only option as history proves Carron is no good at guessing games. He thunders back down the stairs two at a time and joins me on the sofa.

'Sorry about that, but thirteen hours in scrubs and I needed to wash the filth off me before I sit down and relax.' He plants a kiss on the top of my head and pours us a glass of wine. Taking a sip, I debate whether to hit him with it now, or let him finish his dinner first. He's already tucking in, so I leave it until we are done. I don't know whether to love or hate the fact that Carron's life is so full of pleasing others. Because of this I feel like he's missed the moments when he could have perhaps made a difference to our own relationship.

'This is delicious… did you change the recipe again?'

'No, I probably just added a little too much sour cream.'

'Well it's your best yet, don't change this one, okay?'

'You got it,' I say feebly. Carron is animated through dinner, although he looks completely shagged. His new role is taking a while for him to get used to, the hours in particular. His normally bright eyes have bags underneath them and his facial hair is a little longer than usual. We finish our meals and Carron sits back comfortably on the sofa and rubs his flat belly.

'That was excellent – my compliments to the chef.' He drinks what is left of his wine and flicks through the television channels. I need to grab a breather before I launch into my news.

'I'm just going to load the dishwasher.'

'Thanks, honey. I'll be right here.' He smiles and fills his glass with a little more wine. I make a hasty retreat back to the kitchen and dump the plates on the bench. *You can do this,* I tell myself. I scrape my leftovers into the bin, being too nervous to eat much, and load them into the dishwasher. The scotch beckons me from the cabinet and I scull another couple of mouthfuls. No more stalling. The time has come. Time to go rip my friend's heart out of his chest and kick it to him like it's nothing. I'm sure I just vomited a little in my mouth. I square my shoulders, take a deep breath and burst through the door to the living room.

I stop dead in my tracks. Shit.

The background noise of the game show that is playing on the television screen does nothing to block out the noise of Carron's contented snores. I sag. The let-down is unbearable and my knees start to shake. I lurch forward to the couch and fall against the seat. Carron is completely out cold and unaware of my movements next to him. He continues to sleep, blissfully unaware of the heartache I was just about to inflict upon him. Tears prick my eyes and there is nothing I can do to stop the flow as they trickle down my cheeks. They're hot and wet, flowing like a river racing to the ocean. I brush them away frantically with the back of my hand, little sobs forming in the back of my throat.

I want to be numb, so fucking numb that I just don't have to feel anything right now. The wine bottle beckons me and I pour a full glass and scull it quickly. Finishing it does nothing. I know I'm going to need a lot more than that. Refilling the red liquid into my glass just about empties the bottle. Drinking it starts to make my head fuzzy and my body tingly but, annoyingly, my feelings just will not leave me tonight.

A blanket hangs over the side of the arm of the couch and I reach for it, dragging it over Carron and me. I turn the television off and plunge the room into darkness. I find Carron's hand and take it in mine. Leaning against him, my body succumbs to the sleep that has already taken him. Thankfully dreams stay at bay, and I am afforded rest that doesn't inflict guilt or pain. It doesn't last though. Everybody has to wake up some time or another.

Twenty-Four

I never did get the chance to speak to Carron. Work consumes him, as guilt does me. Lyra gives me knowing glances and sometimes raises her eyebrows at me, wanting to know if I have done the decent thing yet and told Carron the truth. The fact is, there really hasn't been the right time.

All week he has been working late so I have kept on moving with my plans and have been packing boxes with stuff I want to take. They get left in the spare room of the house. I'm sure if Carron discovers them there I will have some explaining to do, but part of me wants to be found out. At least then I wouldn't have to actually let those horrid words leave my lips.

My car is booked in for a service so it can be checked over before I make the trip to Maryland. I purchase a cat carrier for Jezebel, who is coming with me. It seems kind of unfair that I am not even leaving the cat to keep him company. Bills are paid and I transfer the electricity and telephone line into Carron's name. There seems like not much else to do, except get in my car and drive away.

Two days before Angel is due to meet me I receive an email from him just before I leave work.

To: bails@quickmail.com
From: thurmontlumberyard@wizzmail.net

Subject: Is your heart beating as fast as mine?
Two days. I'm suffocating with anticipation. Finally I am coming to get you. Be waiting for me Bails…
Angel.

I quickly tap out a reply.

To: thurmontlumberyard@wizzmail.net
From: bails@quickmail.com
Subject: With bells on
Need I say more LOL.
Bails xx

The second I press send it shoots down the Ethernet and heads to where Angel is awaiting my reply in Thurmont. I picture him in his wood cabin, *our* wood cabin now, and smiling at my reply. His dark eyes will crinkle in delight and my heart swells at the thought. James and Lyra are in the office late today, so I leave them to lock up and turn off the computers.

It's blisteringly cold outside tonight and I can smell snow in the air, which means we are sure to have some ice in the not too distant future. As I hurry along the footpath in the direction of home, I'm aware of a car slowing on the road behind me. Turning I glance a set of headlights flashing me and I stop to allow Carron to pull up beside me.

'Hey, stranger, want a lift?' His grin is infectious.

'Sure.' Sliding in the passenger seat, I am suddenly enveloped in warmth. The car heater is cranked up high and Carron has the radio on low.

'Just as well I spotted you. It's supposed to rain tonight.'

'I thought it smelled like snow.'

'Probably not quite cold enough.'

'Feels it.'

'That's probably because you've been snuggled up warm as a bug in that office all day.'

'True.'

'What shall we do about tea tonight?'

'Do you mind if we just get pizza ordered in?'

'I don't think you will have to twist my arm,' he says with a grin. 'But I reckon I'll have a beer with it.' We drive on in silence, letting the music drift between us.

Dinner is enjoyed in comfortable silence, and by now I am fully aware that I will not utter a single word to Carron before I leave. I can't bring myself to do it and I take the chicken's way out by deciding to leave him a note. Tonight is peaceful, and I enjoy his easy company for what it is. He's always been my friend, the one who has comforted me when Angel has been distant and unwilling to pursue our relationship further. Now that Angel is ready to finally accept our relationship, it's time to let the security blanket go and give myself completely to the man who has always held my heart in his hands.

For the first time since I have been back, we head up to bed together. Under normal circumstances, a couple in this situation would make love. My head does terrible things with that thought. If I sleep with Carron, am I not being unfaithful to Angel? If I don't sleep with Carron, will he suspect something is up? I let him use the bathroom first and then take my time, hoping he will be asleep by the time I make it to the bed, removing the decision making process altogether.

Tonight he definitely wants to be together. There is no avoiding him as I slip between the sheets. His body is already naked and he creeps towards me, seeking my mouth out in the dark. We both lay on our sides as we kiss tenderly – not passionately. I feel his erection against my thigh, but a part of my brain has already put up a barrier, forcefully telling me no.

'Ah, Carron?'

'Mmm?'

'I have my period.' *Goddamn fucking liar.*

'That's okay, honey,' he murmurs against my neck as he continues to nuzzle me. There is no putting him off, but I indulge him in other ways. I slink lower under the covers and push him onto his back. My lips trail down his hairy belly and find the tip of his cock. Taking him in my mouth I hear him moan, pleased that I'm paying him service.

Working my mouth I bring him closer to orgasm. It has been so long between us that I don't need to invest too much into the action. He comes quickly and I aim his semen to the back of my throat where I don't have to taste it. My eyes water and I hold back the gagging reflex as his shaft spasms against the back of my mouth. Spent and sated, he pulls me up into his arms and cuddles me. All I want to do is cry, but I don't.

I know I should be happy that I am finally getting what I want. All I've ever wanted is Angel; I know this to be true. But there is something inside of me, deep in the pit of my heart, locked away so I can't quite touch it or feel it. Kind of like when a person's arm has been amputated after they have had use of it all their lives. Even though it is now gone, they sometimes still feel what it was like to have it there. In this instant I'm shocked to realize that perhaps I have unwittingly allowed a small part of Carron access to my heart after all.

Twenty-Five

The light filters through the blinds, so I know it must be later in the morning. I've slept in, but I'm kind of happy about that. At least I won't have to face Carron. He's left for the hospital early again. Angel's email yesterday indicated he would be here around 11:00 a.m., which judging by the bedside clock means I have about two hours until he arrives. I am ready. All of my stuff is packed to go. The only thing left to do is write Carron a letter. After organizing everything else, I knew this is going to be the hardest thing I would have to do.

Groaning, I roll out of bed and hit the shower straight away. I lather my hair with shampoo and repeat the process twice, massaging out the stress I can feel building. Today is going to be one of the most monumental days of my life and, as excited as I am, the little nagging in the back of my head is not allowing me to fully enjoy it. There's something I'm missing, but I try not to let it worry me.

The towel does a decent job of drying my hair, but I finish it off with the hair dryer. Knowing I have a long drive ahead of me, I dress in comfortable clothes and tie my hair up in a braid. I head down to the kitchen and feed Jez before fixing myself a strong cup of coffee and some toast with jam. There is a pen and paper next to the phone and I grab these as I sit down at the table to write. I take a long sip of coffee and compose myself, willing the right words to come to me.

Dear Carron,

Sweet, sweet Carron. There's nothing I can really say to make any of this easier on you, but I can honestly tell you that hurting you is the last thing I ever wanted to do. The day we met, I wasn't even sure if anything would come out of our relationship, but you surprised me with your kindness and compassion. You loved me, despite all my faults. You loved, without ever expecting to be loved in return, and for that I am forever grateful.

I don't know if you know this, but at the time, you kind of saved me. You brought me out of despair when I was so miserable and lost. I know you don't know the reason why I was this way, and even now I can't tell you. But you made a difference, and that is what I want you to know. You made my life happy again.

You probably wonder why I have left… that's just it – I'm leaving. I'm sad to leave you but, if I am honest, I don't think I could ever really make you fully happy because I wouldn't ever be able to fully give myself to you. This is because I belonged to someone else a long time before I met you. I have tried to love you as much as you love me, but I hate to say, my heart has fallen short.

Because of this I feel, to be fair to both of us, I need to call our relationship and engagement off. I'm sorry I lack the courage to tell you this in person but I feel it is for the best, because I believe you would try and convince me to stay and I know that I can't.

I want you to be happy and be loved in a way you deserve – I truly hope a woman worthy of you will come into your life.

I will always cherish the time we have spent together and will never forget you.

Please don't try to find me or contact me… it's better this way. Nothing good can come from being with me except for more disappointment. I want you to stay on at the house if you like. I have put the bills in your name so if you choose to leave you can just cancel the utilities without any hassle. I have contacted the bank and left you written instructions for rent to go straight into the mortgage account. If there is any emergency with the house please leave a message with Lyra and she will be sure to get it to me.

I think it is best if we have no contact, it will be just like rubbing salt into an already open wound and I would hate to give you false hope of a reunion.

As much as this will hurt you, I have to be honest and tell you that as much as I love you, I'm not in love with you. Another man stole my heart a long time ago and I cannot change that. This is the reason I'm leaving. It is too unfair for me to be with you when you give yourself to me so selflessly and I do nothing but use you up because I am too weak to be on my own. Feeble, I know, but there it is.

I wish you every success with your career and pray that someone deserving of your love will bring you the happiness I know I can never give you.

Love,

Bailey x

I'm crying now, big fat tears sliding helplessly down my cheeks. I fold the letter and slip it under the kettle on the kitchen bench and then go to the bathroom and splash water on my face. I apply some makeup and try to look a little less like shit. The red eyes can't be fixed, but I do my best with what I have. Keeping busy until it is time to go will take my mind off Carron, so I go to the spare room and start moving the small boxes to the back door where I know Angel will back the truck up to. There is still an hour to go and I have finished doing everything I possibly can.

Deciding another cup of coffee is just what I need to settle my nerves I brew a fresh jug and seat myself on the couch with Jezebel and flick on the morning news program. They alternate between news, entertainment, cooking segments and interviews. I pay no attention to any of it. My mind sees the images, but nothing registers. I'm too wired to allow my brain to focus.

11:00 a.m. comes and goes. I rinse my mug and put it in the sink before taking up occupancy in the front window seat. My eyes watch the road like a hawk, but still no truck comes. I hope that Angel won't be too late, just in case Carron decides to come home for lunch. *How awkward would that be?*

I keep checking my watch. A quarter past. Half past. Still no Angel. Fed up, I return to the living room just as the news bulletin flashes on the screen. The reporter informs viewers of headlining news that is just breaking. Suddenly I find myself turning the volume up to maximum, transfixed as words spill out of her mouth. She's reporting from the Astoria side of the Astoria-Megler Bridge.

'NBNC is coming to you live from Astoria with breaking news of a multi-vehicle accident that has not long since taken place on the Astoria-Megler Bridge. Reports currently indicate a 96 ton gas tanker has slid across several lanes on the bridge, ice being a major factor in the road conditions. It is unclear at this stage if there any fatalities, but authorities currently indicate at least five other vehicles have been involved and one smaller truck. We will stay live here on the scene and bring you the very latest information as it comes to light. Back to you in the studio…'

My blood runs cold and the phone ringing in the kitchen startles me out of my trance. I race to grab it, slipping on the rug as I bang my shin on the corner of the coffee table. The kitchen clock strikes midday, I grab the receiver out of its cradle and press it firmly to my ear, knuckles turning white as I grip it.

'Hello?' *Please be Angel. Please be Angel. Oh dear God, I will fucking do anything. Anything in this world if you just let him be okay.*

'Bailey?' Carron's voice comes over loud and clear in the receiver. He doesn't sound like himself though. He sounds funny. I can barely choke out a reply. My tongue has ceased to work and I feel like I have a handful of cotton balls stuck in the back of my throat.

'Yes…' Silence hangs between us. 'Yes,' I repeat.

'Honey, I ah…'

'Yes?' I swallow nervously. I am capable of nothing more; it's all I can summon. There is nothing else.

'There's been a big accident on the bridge.' *I fucking know! Just tell me goddamn it, get it over with for Christ's sake!*

'Yes…'

'You better get down to the hospital right now.' He sounds utterly miserable. His voice is struck with sorrow, something I've never heard before. *Fuck, this must be bad.*

'Yes…'

'Honey, I'm sorry. I didn't know your brother was coming to visit you today. He was in his truck on the bridge when a tanker flipped and clipped his rear. Look, he's in a bad way and the whole hospital is in chaos. I'm needed and have to go help with treating him. I just quickly slipped away to call you so you could come down, you know, just in case he doesn't make it…' his voice trails off. When I say nothing he says, 'Bails, are you there?'

'I'm here.'

'Did you hear what I just said?'

'Yes.'

'Can you drive yourself down or do you want me to call a cab for you?'

There is a pause before I snap myself out of it.

'I'm on my way.' I drop the receiver to the floor without hanging up and grab my car keys from next to the kettle. The letter to Carron is there and I snatch it up as I run at a dead sprint for the back door.

Twenty-Six

As soon as I hit the downward run of the hill towards the hospital I can see smoke pluming near the bridge. From here things don't look good. My driving is crazy, I'm like a woman possessed and anything in my way is going to get beeped, swerved around and cussed at. There is only one focus, and that is Angel.

'No! No, no, nooooo!' I bang my hand on the steering wheel so hard I almost snap my wrist. 'Oh my God, please no. I will do anything, anything you hear me?'

My prayers force me to think I am being punished. Have I been so bad, so wrong with my judgment that God is stepping in and taking him from me? Why me? *Oh fuck. Please, please let him be okay. Wait for me Angel,* I plead.

I swing the car into the hospital driveway and double park it out the front of the emergency doors. I don't even turn off the engine – I just leave the car running there with the keys in.

'Miss? Miss! You can't leave that car parked there!' *Yeah? Just watch me, buddy.* I sprint away from where the security guard is approaching and barrel my way through the front doors of emergency.

'Carron? Carron!' I'm yelling for him, despite the fact I have no knowledge of his whereabouts. 'Carron!' I'm almost sobbing now and desperate for someone to rescue me before

I fall to pieces in the middle of the waiting room. A group of nurses come running towards me and I half expect one of them to inject me with something to sedate me like they do in psych wards. They don't though.

'Are you Bailey?' A large African-American nurse asks me.

'Yes,' I sob.

'Come with me, child. Carron's up on the third floor preparing the operating theatre for surgery.' She takes my hand and leads me to the bank of elevators. A car arrives shortly and she pulls me inside, stabbing her long fake nail on the third floor button. She squeezes my hand, sure that I need the reassurance. I do, and I'm grateful for the gesture. *Please, God, I'll do anything remember? I'll even break it off with Angel if that's what you want, just don't let him die! Please!*

We step out as the doors open and hurry down the fluorescent-lit hallway to the operating theatres. She pushes through the first set of doors and hands me a mask to put on and tells me to wash my hands. I quickly do as I'm told knowing time is of the essence. There is another set of doors we go through before we spot Carron talking to a group of doctors. He sees us the instant we walk through the door and he rushes to me and holds me in his arms. As always, Carron does what he does best. He comforts me.

'I'm so sorry, Bailey; I didn't know Emmett was coming down today.' He is apologetic. If only he knew.

'What's happening, Carron? Is he going to make it?'

'We don't know. The Neurological Surgeon has just arrived and he's going to do everything in his power to save him, honey.'

'Can I see him?' I sob. My tears know no bounds today. They stream endlessly, falling unhindered down my face and pool onto the linoleum floor.

'They're about to start surgery. He has a massive head trauma and they need to release pressure on the brain.'

'Please, Carron,' I beg, 'just two seconds is all I need.' He nods, understanding.

'Just a minute.' He leaves me while he consults with the surgeon who is sterilizing his hands at the basin. I note the nod of the surgeon's head as he glances towards me. A flutter of hope flies in my chest and I say a prayer of thanks. I feel if I can just speak to Angel he will hear my voice and come back to me.

Carron motions for me to follow him through to the theatre. He places scrubs over my clothes and slips material over my shoes. We hurry, very aware of the time frame we have. Inside the bright lights glare back at my eyes, assaulting my senses and making me blink rapidly to shrink my pupils fast enough so I can see properly. There are nurses everywhere, organizing the medical equipment that looks more like butcher's tools than a doctor's. My eyes come to rest on the bed in the middle of the room and my heart stops.

I'm still breathing, still alive. But I'm sure my heart stops. Just one little thud that kicks it back into gear again and then I move. So slowly, but I move. Angel is here. I am here. My world is okay again, if only for a moment. I take an unsteady breath. It's enough to get me bedside. I fall beside him.

His eyes are taped shut, and there is blood smeared all over his eyebrows that runs down towards his ears. His cheeks are puffy and as my eyes sweep over his body I notice his leg is bent at a funny angle. I chance a glance at Carron.

'It's broken, but it's the least of their concerns.' I nod, understanding the brain injury is the most serious of his wounds. I turn back to Angel's face and want to place feather-light kisses all over his sweet face.

'Can I have a second?' I don't turn around to see Carron's reaction, but he answers me.

'Sure. I'll go and tell the doctor we're just about finished.'

Bending next to Angel, I pull my mask down a fraction so I can speak to him.

'Angel? It's Bails, Angel. I'm here. I'm here. Can you hear me? I love you, do you know that? I love you so much. I'm never leaving you, okay? I'm going to be standing right outside that door until you wake up. I'm never leaving you; I love you so damn much.' My voice breaks and I cry, not able to continue even if I wanted to.

To the nurses still in the room, I probably sound like a concerned family member. Only Angel and I know the truth. Only we know how deep our love really goes.

The doors to the theatre open and a team of surgeons walk in. Masks cover their faces and their hands are gloved up. Nothing about this seems right, but that probably has something to do with the fact I'm supposed to be on my way to Thurmont to start my new life with Angel. And yet, here we are.

Carron leads me out of the room as they seal the doors. Angel's fate now rests in their hands. I wonder who the surgeons will be today – the super heroes or the villains?

Twenty-Seven

Here I am staring at his perfection and yet my eyes won't let me believe it. He's not out of the woods yet, but my heart won't let go. Not until he takes his last breath. I will keep holding on as long as he does. Surgery was an exhausting seven hours, and when he comes out I station myself bedside, refusing to leave even when the call of nature persists with my discomfort.

Carron and a ward wheeled him into the Intensive Care Unit and left me to my solitary vigil. I know it won't last; soon my parents will be here and I will have to share the little cocoon I have built around us. My chair is pulled up tight to his bed and I rest my head against the edge while I stare at his beautiful face. Even with a fresh scar that runs from his nose to his jaw, he is still the best thing I have ever laid eyes on.

We are alone, finally able to touch but only because the gravity of the circumstance permits this kind of public display of affection. I caress his hand, hoping he can feel my touch. His room is the last on the ward where widows afford a view over the bay. It reminds me of when our parents took us out on a boat there while we were here on vacation. I was ten at the time, he thirteen. We had wetsuits and life jackets on, but it was the first time we were going sailing. I was terrified. Watching *Jaws* at a friend's house when I was six had scared the living shit out of me. The deep dark depths of the ocean made me not want to even dip a big toe in. Without me saying a word, he knew. He protected me. We sat together on the canvass while Mom worked the spinnaker and Dad the sails. He held me tight as we crested the waves and I thought I would fall off into the sea. I was so scared, yet he was my savior even then.

I think back to the day he came to join our family. Even though I was still a baby myself, I knew later that I was resentful at the prospect of having to share my parents with someone else's brat. I mean, he wasn't my *real* brother. But thankfully that has been my saving grace in adulthood – that I can justify our relationship because we're not blood related. Anyone else would have serious issues with this because for all intents and purposes, we've been raised as brother and sister since we were just small children. We were taught to be kind and protect one another, not fuck each other and have a sexual relationship. Our parents would be mortified if they ever found out.

I never saw him as my brother, though. Not that I saw him as a love interest either, but from a young age he was always just Emmett, my friend. We were complete opposites. I was the wallflower, shy and introverted—the bookworm who couldn't get enough of Shakespeare and literature of any kind. Would you believe me if I told you my favorite was Romeo and Juliet? Damn. It was his too. But this side of him never saw the light of day. He was always the popular kid. Great at sports, admired and liked by males and females equally. His dark and broody looks always earned him the interest of every girl in school, but he always ignored them in favor of hanging out with me on the weekends.

That's why there were so many people ready to bash me that day. The other girls who joined Alva in attacking me thought I was in Angel's ear, telling him not to go out with them. They were starting to wonder why he repeatedly refused and ignored all their attention. They implied he was frigid and said they would spread it all over school. I knew I had no chance of taking any of them on, but I'd be damned if they would insult Angel as well as me and get away with it. Even though Alva let fly the first punch, I gave the best fight I had.

Despite the fact I ended up on the ground in a bloody, bruised mess, not in a million years would I take it back. The sheer relief at seeing Angel fly at them made my heart soar. His big strong arms swept me up and took me home. As we left the oval we both caught sight of the mortified look on Coach Sawyer's face. We don't know how long he had been there, but obviously long enough.

Mr. Sawyer didn't say a word to Emmett as he walked off with me. He looked after me. Cared for me. Made love to me. It was a relief to finally love him in the way I wanted to. Suddenly our relationship made sense that day. He felt exactly the same way I did. Of course he struggled with the morality of our relationship more than I did. He even moved to Thurmont to escape prying eyes of the townsfolk from our hometown. Words like incest would be thrown around if anyone ever caught us together. He wouldn't smear my name like that so he called our relationship off after he moved because the guilt still followed him.

I wasn't the same then. My heart broke into a thousand tiny pieces and I couldn't eat, drink or sleep – shit, I could barely breathe without him. That's when I ran into Carron. He made it a little easier to live without Angel. But only for a while. Soon the Band-Aid wasn't enough and my every thought turned back to being consumed by him again until he allowed me to see him again. It was bliss. Perfection. We were born to be together and I just needed to convince him we could live in the real world and still have a relationship without being judged.

Finally our chance had come and now Angel may not make it through this. Fate is a cruel and heartless mistress and I was starting to resent that my opportunity was being ripped out from underneath my feet.

'Please come back to me Angel, I love you so much.' It's a whisper I want to shout. I want him to wake, but I know the drug-induced coma will see him sleep like the dead for several weeks. Just thinking this when Emmett is so close to death brings on a fresh torrent of tears. The doctors have said it is a fifty-fifty chance that he will pull through. Those odds sound shit, but middle of the road is where I have spent most of my life. If he pulls through this I'm going to change that. There is not a single second of our tomorrow that I am going to waste.

A ward kindly brings me a meal, knowing I will not be leaving Emmett's bedside. It is a kind gesture, but I can't force myself to get anything down. How can I eat when the man I love just lies there listlessly in front of me? My eyes watch his face like a hawk, looking for any trace of movement across his eyelids. Does he know I am here? Can he feel me? Will he dream? I send a silent prayer to God, hoping that if he does they are peaceful, resting him and healing his wounds so that he can come back to me better than before. My eyelids start to get heavy and I succumb to closing them, hoping that somewhere in our state of unconscious we will meet again.

Twenty-Eight

I feel a big, warm hand on my shoulder and, as I struggle to wake, I mistakenly think it is Angel. My guardian angel, back to be with me. My eyes flutter open and I am hit with a crick in my neck from sleeping at a funny angle against the bed. I take in his body, which still lies there listlessly, unmoved from when I observed him yesterday. I swivel and see my dad standing behind me. It is his warmth I can feel on my shoulder. His eyes are red and he looks as tortured as I feel.

'Oh Dad,' I sob as I throw myself into his arms. He bear hugs me and comforts me in a way only a father can. He protects his little girl from all the hurt she is feeling, while wishing he could have done the same for his son.

'He's a tough cookie, kiddo, you know that. He's going to pull through, Bails.'

'I hope so, Dad, I don't know what I'll do if he doesn't.' I know that this is a little too close to showing the rawness of my feelings but I am beyond caring.

'Just keep praying, it's all any of us can do.'

'Where's Mom?' A sniffle comes from my nose and I dry my eyes on my tracksuit sleeve.

'She's just gone to get us coffee. Have you eaten?' he asks as he eyes the uneaten meal from last night.

'No,' I say sheepishly, 'but I just can't stomach anything right now.'

'You have to eat, sweetheart. If you go getting sick it's not going to help your brother any. He needs you strong to help him pull through.' Internally I cringe when I hear him call Emmett my brother. I hate it.

'Sure, Dad, I will. Just not right now, okay?'

'Okay, but soon, kiddo.' His voice is gruff and I can tell he is struggling to keep it together as well. We are interrupted by my mom who comes back into the room laden with takeaway coffee cups in hand. I rush to her and embrace her warmth while Dad relieves her of the beverages.

'Oh, honey! Emmett will be okay, I just know he will.'

'How do you know? What makes you so sure?' I'm full on bawling now, not caring in the slightest how emotional I am.

'Because I know that Emmett is a fighter, he always gets what he wants. You should know that better than anyone, honey.' She smiles warmly at me and I'm shocked to think I am reading more into her words than I should be.

'Still…'

'Still nothing. He won't give up without a fight, and he needs you to be strong right now. Why don't you head home and get some rest while your dad and I are here.'

'I can't leave him, Mom.'

'You're going to need a nice warm shower and a fresh set of clothes, honey. Go now, and we'll call you if anything happens.'

'But what if I'm not here, and…' My voice trails off, unable to finish my sentence. I can't even begin to think what would happen if he took a turn for the worse and I wasn't here to be with him.

'Nonsense! Us Michaels are built of stronger stuff than that, Bailey. Go now, and come back after you've had a rest.'

'Okay, but call me the minute anything happens, no matter how big or small. I won't be long.'

'Don't you worry now.' My mother kisses my cheeks and my dad embraces me in another bear hug.

'Thanks, I'll see you later.' I'm nearly at the door when my mom calls back after me.

'Bailey, your jacket's over on the chair there. Carron left it for you before he headed home this morning. Poor guy, I think he was absolutely exhausted.'

'Thanks.' I grab it; a sudden ill feeling washes over me. My parents wave goodbye and I step into the hallway of the ICU ward. My hands find the pockets of the jacket as I shrug it on. I double check. The note I had written to Carron has gone from the pocket I placed it in yesterday on my way to the hospital. *Fuck*. I guess I have some explaining to do.

The nurse's station on the ground floor provides me with my car keys and they inform me the security detail has parked my car in the hospital's parking garage on the second floor. In a trance I find it and gun the engine, tearing off towards home to receive the punishment I know I so sorely deserve.

Twenty-Nine

I drive furiously. There is a part of me that knows I'm going to need to comfort Carron and a part that has enough sense to know I am going to need to beg for forgiveness. This early, the traffic is slow. Kids have already been dropped off at school and moms and dads have already started their day jobs. It doesn't take long. My car finds its place at the top of the driveway and I sit a moment as the engine still ticks over. Carron's car is parked in front of me and I don't need any other sign that he is already home.

The fact that he hasn't called me is a clear indicator that I am in big trouble. Never before has he ignored me, not bothered to call me or communicate with me in some way – especially not for more than a day. I pull the keys and undo my seatbelt, step out of the car and head towards the rear kitchen door. Tentatively I push it open. It's not locked, although I didn't expect it to be.

The kitchen is empty and dark. It's a miserable day and I suppose it suits all of our moods just fine. Baby steps find me in the living room. The television is on, but the sound is muted. The sight before me is haunting, but to be honest, I didn't know how it could get any worse than how I see it right now. As much as I tried to avoid all this, I still see a broken man before me. He sits in the darkness, the shades drawn to keep out any residual light. He's staring at the coffee table, and in front of him is the piece of paper I had written the letter to him on the day before. I know he knows I am here, yet he says nothing. His hands find his head, covering his face and trying to ward off any more hurt that I could possibly inflict on him.

'Carron?' He says nothing and I'm suddenly scared that he may be so traumatized that he can no longer be responsive to anyone.

'Carron? Please, Carron, can you just look at me. Please.' Slowly I track my way around the sofa so I am standing in front of him. He doesn't move, but I sit myself down on the coffee table and ignore the letter, placing my ass down on top of it so that I am sitting directly in front of him. If he would only lift his eyes he would be staring directly into mine. I feel guilty for asking anything of him right now and I get the feeling I am going to need to convince him a little more before I can get his attention.

'Carron, please, can we talk?' He is silent a moment before he drinks me in, taking the time to fully appraise me for probably the first time in his life.

'What's to talk about? I think your letter says it all, don't you?' His tone is not even the least bit bitter and I hate myself that I have caused such a beautiful man so much heartache.

'I'm so sorry, there's no excuse.' His eyes blaze, ready for a fight.

'You're right. There really isn't. I have done nothing but love you so damn much, Bailey – offering you love, security, honesty and friendship. And this is how you repay me? Really? Because I never in a million years thought that you could inflict so much pain on another human being. I thought you were one of the good ones; I thought you gave a shit. I thought you were the one who needed saving and loving. Obviously I was so wrong. It was me, wasn't it? I really needed saving from someone like you.'

'Carron, please…'

'See, even though you are begging for me to listen to you, it will only be to tell me what you have already written. There is no changing your mind, changing you. I see that now. It never was me, was it?'

'I…'

'Tell me the truth damn it!' His shouts reach me and tear right through my heart. I never wanted any of this.

'No. It has never been you.' That is as honest as I can get and I know he damn well deserves the truth after all I have put him through.

'It's him? Your own damn brother?'

'I don't see him like that Carron.'

'Obviously not, or you wouldn't have been sneaking behind my back all this time now would you?'

'If there was anything I could take back, Carron, it would be this. You were never meant to get hurt, and I never meant to continue a relationship with Emmett.'

'But you did, right under my nose. What a fool I have been!'

'No! You're not the fool – I am! To not realize what a wonderful man you are. I should never have continued to see you, but there was something about you that brought me such comfort.'

'Oh, I see. Well I am so glad that I could be a fill-in for your *brother*.' I flinch at the harshness of his tone.

'You never were a fill-in, Carron.' But even I don't believe the words that are coming out of my mouth.

'Right. The letter says it all plainly here, Bails. It has always been him, and always will be. Isn't that right? Be honest, it's always been him who you're really in love with isn't it?' I can't believe for the first time in my life I am about to admit this to another human being. But it is all there. All on the table to lay bare.

'Yes.' My words are just a whisper that linger on the still air like a repugnant smell.

'I'm sorry, I don't think I heard you the first time.'

'Yes! Damn it, yes! It has always been him. There is nothing I could do to change that, despite how hard I have tried. But you have to believe me when I say, that you were the last person on this earth that I wanted to hurt.'

'Really? Is that why you were going to leave without saying a word? Without giving me the honesty I deserve.'

'I'm a chickenshit, I know it Carron. Please believe me when I tell you that I love you, I always have.'

'But you're not in love with me are you? Isn't that what you said?'

'You're right, I'm in love with Emmett. There is nothing on this earth that will change that. Believe me, I've tried.'

'So that leaves me high and dry?'

'I was hoping it would afford you the opportunity to find your soul mate, without being baggaged with all my shit.'

'You know what, Bailey? I have always known you were damaged. I just never realized how bad. Truth is, you were

206

my soul mate in my eyes. There wasn't a single woman on this earth that I would rather be with.' His words crush me. The devastation is far worse than I had ever intended. Tears start to form in his eyes and I lean forward, as if to try to wipe them from the corners. He pulls back, not allowing my touch to reach him anymore.

'Carron, I...'

'There's nothing left to say, Bailey. You've said it all. It's not like anything I say is going to convince you to stay with me, is it?'

'No.' It's harsh, but the truth.

'Well I guess I'm the sore loser then, aren't I? Looks like Emmett had you all stitched up before I even came along.'

'Please, Carron. It's not like that.'

'My ass it's not! Do you know how sick that is? You may not be blood related, but your parents certainly raised you both to be siblings.' Horror spreads across my face. It suddenly occurs to me that perhaps in his angered state he might reveal our relationship to others.

'You can't tell anyone, Carron.'

'No?'

'I mean it, you can't. It would hurt so many people.'

'So I'm the only one who is supposed to suffer?'

'That's not what I wanted!' I reach forward to grab him, hug him. At first he pushes me away, angered that I would dare touch him.

'Don't try to console me, Bailey. You've done enough.' His words catch in the back of his throat and his anguish hits me in waves. I fight him, struggling to hold him close so that he can let go of all his anger he feels towards me. He pulls my hair back and looks into my eyes with despair.

'I love you so much, you know?'

'I know, and I don't deserve you. I never have.' I hug him and hold him tight as he falls apart. Tonight I will hold him so close, but in the morning I know I will have to let him go for good. This isn't healthy for any of us, least of all Carron. He sobs – not like any other man I have ever seen. It breaks my heart more than anything I have ever seen so far in my young life. Not because I care so much, but because I have cared so little. This is one life I did not intend to ruin.

Finally the despair subsides and we both cling to each other. Familiarity, friendship and time are what bond us together as we both deal with our grief.

While I'm dying to get back to the hospital to Angel, a telephone call to my mom assures me there has been no change. Right now, I know Carron needs me more. We don't exchange any more words, for it will only bring more tears and sadness. The only thing left for both of us is to accept the circumstances we have been thrown into. I *need* him to come to terms with our break-up before I can move on.

By morning, an unspoken resolve has formed.

'I need to go to the hospital. I checked in with Mom last night and Emmett seems to be the same, but I need to go see him.'

'Sure, you go. I won't be far behind you.'

'You're not going to say anything are you?' I'm hesitant to ask, but I need to hear him say the words. He looks at me, disbelief written all over his face.

'Do you really think so little of me?'

'I... no...'

'I may not approve or agree with your relationship with your brother at all in this lifetime, Bailey, but there will never be anything that will make me betray the trust you hold in me. You have my word – no one will ever know your secret from my mouth. All I ever wanted was for you to be happy.' I rush him, throwing my arms around him for what could very well be the last time.

'Thank you, Carron. Oh thank you!' His arms don't wrap around me like they normally do, and his actions don't go unnoticed by me. The nail in our relationship coffin has been firmly hammered in. There is no undoing it. It is time to go to the man who is waiting for me. The one I have loved all along. The one I knew I was born to be with. I place a gentle kiss on his cheek and resolve forms on his features. Even though he has bared himself to me, I'm betting I have no real idea of the torment I have caused him.

Without another word I pick up my keys and leave him. I can feel his eyes on me, but I never look back. This part of my journey can only go forward, so I close the door behind me and head to my car. Despite the sadness I feel for Carron, my heart feels lighter. Finally I am free to be with one man.

Angel, I'm coming for you, darling.

I say a silent prayer that I'm not too late to bring the man I love back from the dead.

Thirty

The days and weeks in the hospital are tough. Emmett remains in an induced coma to allow his brain a better chance at recovering from his injuries. I stay vigilant: nothing else matters. I become a shell of my former self. Food becomes a distraction, only ever eaten at the insistence of Carron or my parents. My job takes a dive and Maria is notified by Lyra that I am taking an extended leave of absence.

Lyra knows something is up with Emmett and I, but I think even she is not willing to let her brain go there yet.

Carron does what he always does. He supports me. Sure the pain, hurt and anger linger – of course they would. But as always he is a big enough person to put aside his own anguish to focus on my happiness. He told me he can't stay mad at me for long, which only makes me feel even more guilty for taking advantage of him all the time we've been together.

My days become a new sort of routine. I shower at home and then drive to the hospital. Emmett lays there like sleeping beauty, hopefully unaware of all the people who are upset that he is still not out of the woods. I stay by his side, talking to him and recounting all my favorite times we've spent together. I actually smile when I reminisce about the time he took me ice skating. Like all sports, he was very good at it, but to make me feel better about my own clumsiness he pretended to keep slipping and falling over. By the end of our outing I was in stitches. It was the most childish carefree fun I had ever experienced, and all he did was try to make me feel better about myself. That's what I have always adored about Angel – he always made me feel that I was so much more than I ever thought I was. He made me love myself and gave me the confidence I sorely lacked. He made me feel beautiful and confident, instilling in me the confidence to grow into adulthood and feel like I was worthy. Not just of him, but of everything and everyone. He was, and always will be, my anchor.

Mom and Dad settle into a routine with me. When they arrive in the evening, I kiss Emmett's cheek, promising I will be back the next morning. Mom takes over, loves him, spoils him and talks to him. Dad is a passive visitor. He's feeling just as much as the rest of us, yet in his time of grief he's still not able to fully let himself go.

***

The house is quiet; Carron has moved out. I begged him to stay, knowing my life would not be in Astoria anytime in the near future, but he told me there were too many memories in the house. Eddy offered to have him at his place, so he packed up his stuff and moved out.

If I told you I didn't cry, I would be lying. It hurt like a bitch. My security blanket had finally been snatched from me. There was no comfort waiting at home, but as much as I knew this was the right thing for Carron, I still missed him.

One night in particular when I was feeling really low, I called him.

Asking him to come over wasn't in the plan, but he comes bearing Chinese takeaway and beer. I glimpse the six pack as he walks in the back door.

'I thought we could both drown our sorrows a bit.' I nod, completely understanding. Shit, if he felt half as lonely as I did then he must have been hurting a lot.

We take the food to the living room and try to involve ourselves in the football match on television. We're not really watching it though; it's just a distraction from conversation. Even though we don't utter a single word all night, deep in my heart I know we will be all right. I hope that in the future we can become friends when all the hurt and lies have had time to fade into the background. Because at the end of all of this, Carron is still my friend. Despite the fact he doesn't know me like Emmett, he still knows me better than any other person I know. His easygoing personality calms me, makes me feel comfortable in my own skin. And now that there is no pressure to love him romantically, I have to admit I feel I want to be closer to him than ever before. It comes down to trust, and if there is one thing I can say with total confidence it's that I trust Carron completely.

We spend the rest of the night drinking and watching the game. Neither of us wants to be alone tonight, so we turn off the television and grab the blanket that is a constant in my living room. We snuggle up on the couch – two people offering each other support while each of us goes through their own turmoil.

In the morning I am wrapped in his arms and I wake feeling the most rested I have in a long time. I feel him stir beneath me, and I shift to release his arm from underneath me. At that moment, the phone in the kitchen starts ringing, as does my cell while Carron's pager starts beeping. We try to answer all at once. The messages are all the same.

Emmett has taken a turn for the worse. He has just suffered a stroke when a blood clot went to his brain. They didn't realize that in the accident his carotid artery had been cut off, causing him to sustain injury. There are other complications also, but I miss most of it with my mom's hysterical wailing. My dad takes the phone and tells us to get to the hospital right now.

I'm a mess; there is no way I can drive. Calm, sensible Carron takes my keys out of my shaking hands, drives us safely to the hospital and drops me out front while he parks. I don't look back as I slam the car door and race for the stairwell. There is no way I am waiting for a lift, instead I take the stairs two at a time to the ICU ward. A bed is in the hallway as I race out of the lift and I collide heavily with it, bruising my kneecap and buckling my legs. I dust myself off and continue racing down towards the end room.

The commotion reaches my ears from here. There are a lot of noises and people shouting and giving orders. My mom's sobbing can be heard in the background. My dad shouts, 'Do something, there must be something you can do!'

The glass wall of the room allows me to see the scene perfectly before I am even in there with them. There are numerous staff in the room, my mom and dad huddled in the corner, a grief stricken expression all over their features.

I'm running for all I am worth, but even now I don't know if I have made it in time. I rush towards the bed, but am shoved heavily back by a ward hand. My eyes dart to the monitor that displays all Angel's stats and I see the last of a visible heartbeat flat line and run off into a straight line on the screen. In that instant, my world stops. It is taken, crushed and stomped on at my feet. God must be playing a cruel joke on me today and I remind him that I promised him anything, just don't let this man die.

'No!' Afterwards I will remember thinking that I am sure everybody in the whole hospital would have heard me cry out. Nurses and doctors rush around me. Emmett's gown is ripped open and they attach the paddles for the defibrillator onto his chest.

'Everybody clear!' The doctor holds his hands up and motions for everyone to move back. I'm forcibly removed away from his bed by a large nurse, intent on not zapping me when they shock Emmett's body. The machine whines and lets out a loud noise as it shocks him violently. His whole body convulses and I look towards the monitor for hope. His heartbeat is still flat lining, so the doctor moves to charge the defibrillator again. All I want to do is crush myself to Angel's body once more.

'Angel, come back to me, come back to me now! God damn it, Emmett, you promised me! You'd never leave. Come back you bastard, come back! You promised!' My tiny fists pummel his chest, although I know the action is doing him no good at all. The nurse grabs me again and I kick out, desperate to be with him one last second. The doctor sees I'm clear and presses the button to charge the machine once more. It whines as it reaches a high pitched frequency.

Once again his body convulses.

Like the rest of the people in the room, my eyes track the monitor. All I need is one little beep on the screen to make my world complete again.

Nothing. Not even the tiniest of spikes. From where I am held, I shout again, as though I'm confident that if I scream loud enough that he will hear me.

'Angel! Please don't leave me. Please, I'm begging you. Come back and be with me!' The fight in me is leaving. My hope is trickling away with every passing second that his heart rate isn't registering on the monitor.

'Clear, one last time,' the doctor orders. Everyone steps back from his body and the paddles are placed on his chest for the last time. It's make or break for Angel.

Please, God. You can't let someone so good die today. I beg you. Please do this for me. I need him! I need him more than anything else on this Earth!

The machine whines. It reaches charge point and the light indicates it is good to go. The doctor places the paddles on his chest and shocks him.

All eyes turn to the monitor.

We watch.

We wait.

And I, more than anyone else in this room, pray that I will see the blip on the monitor that will show me Emmett is still alive and kicking.

Epilogue

It's been a tough year since the accident on the bridge. I've coped with things as best as I could. To be honest, I didn't think I was strong enough to make it through sometimes.

Surprisingly, Carron and I have grown closer. Funny as it sounds, he has done nothing but support me and our friendship has blossomed because of it. It is nice to finally be able to confide in him in the way that I have always wanted to – without the lies.

After all the heartache of the past year, I'm surprised to find myself in Mexico. Cancún is blistering hot this time of year and I plan on getting at least a little color on my pale skin among other things. You see, it's not just a holiday. I'm here to get married. I didn't think I would ever see the end of an aisle, especially after the accident. But here I am.

I've ducked out of the hotel for a six pack of Coronas and some limes. The walk along the beach to the liquor store is calming and refreshing. By 10:00 a.m. tomorrow I'm going to be saying 'I do'. Here, away from home, I feel remarkably calm. With purchases in arm, I dip my feet in the ocean as I make my way back to the hotel room we have rented for a month right on the beachfront.

Work has been good, and they have been very generous in allowing me time to heal – to find myself again. Of course they are not fully aware of the whole story, but my commitment to the company previously has afforded me a little flexibility.

It's late afternoon and the sun is just dipping on the horizon. While heading to the tenth floor, I take the time to gaze at my engagement ring. It's big, and beautiful. It sparkles back at me brilliantly. There is one big diamond in the middle, with lots of little ones trailing off out from the center. It looks like a snowflake. When I made mention of this, I was told that it was a snowflake. My mind drifts back to the conversation we had over it.

'Do you know why a snowflake?'

'No, why?'

'Because no two snowflakes will ever be the same. You are my snowflake, Bailey. Perfectly original and unlike any other woman I have ever known.'

If it's possible, I love him a little more when he says this to me. I smile at the memory. The elevator arrives on our floor and I make my way to our room. In my haste to go out, I left my pass key inside. It's not a problem, because he is here. Smiling, I knock gently on the door. A gush of air rushes at me as it is flung open. He grabs me and pulls me inside.

'God I missed you.' His lips find my neck and I submit by tipping my head back to receive him.

'You always have.'

'And I'm never going to stop either.' The beer is forgotten as we make our way to the bed. We make love. Sweetly, tenderly, passionately. It's the last time we will make love as individuals.

***

I never thought about eloping before. The suggestion made me think that suddenly everything could be a possibility. It is just the two of us. We walk hand in hand to the little gazebo chapel the marriage celebrant has set up on the beach. There is no way I'm going to be late, so we arrive exactly on time.

In the daylight we are on our own. The beach is yet to fill with tourists, despite the sun blaring brilliantly over the ocean. Most will be sleeping off hangovers from the night before, leaving us to feel like we are the only two people on Earth right at this point in time.

As we walk on the sand holding hands, my eyes take in his. I'm lost in the fairytale of a love story that I can hardly believe. Suddenly everything is right with the world. I feel like I can tackle anything with him by my side.

We approach the celebrant, both dressed in white – him in shirt and pants, while I opt for a simple flowing dress. I carry white roses, red twine holding the bunch together.

The celebrant is a round, welcoming Mexican man with a smile as bright as the sun. You can tell he loves his job. His teeth are perfectly white, visible all the while as he keeps smiling at us.

'Welcome! I'm honored that I can join you lovely people in marriage today.'

'Thank you,' we chorus and get lost in each other's eyes again as we face each other.

The celebrant refers to his book.

'Today we are joining two souls who share a commitment with being together for a lifetime in marriage. It is a commitment you have not entered into lightly; it is a commitment that reaffirms your love for each other. Bailey, please read your vows.'

I hold the hands of the man I am about to marry, knowing with every fiber of my being that I am doing the right thing.

'I promise to love and cherish you forever. I give you my soul to keep, to love, to be yours and no other's for as long as we both shall live. I promise that I will be with you and only you, always – through sickness and in health, through poverty and wealth. This I give to you, my vows to be a wife who will never be jealous or unkind. My support will extend to all aspects of your life, and you will always have me to lean on when you need a friend or lover. My heart is yours and I entrust it with you to carry until death do us part.' A single tear slips from the corner of his eye. His lips quiver with restrained control as he reins in his emotions.

'And I promise to love and cherish you forever. My soul belongs to you and only you – to keep, to love and hold for as long as we both shall live. You have proven that you will always be here for me, and I can only hope to offer you the same and more in return. Whether in sickness or health, rich or poor, you are my life, my love and I would die for you. I can't promise that I will never be jealous, but I will try damn hard not to be.'

In my peripheral vision I see the celebrant smile widely. He continues.

'I will never be unkind. My support will extend to all aspects of your life, and you will always have me to lean on when you need a friend or lover. My heart is yours and I entrust it with you to carry until death do us part.'

'And now I pray you have God walk with you both as you take this journey through life as a married couple.' The celebrant refers to his book for a minute as if puzzled for a second. His pause gives us reason to tear our eyes away from each other and look in his direction.

'Sorry,' he apologizes, 'I thought there might be some error with my notes, but it appears not. Do you, Bailey Reagan Michaels, take Emmett Wade Michaels to be your lawful wedded husband?' I giggle as I look from Angel to the celebrant.

'That's quite a coincidence you both already have the same surname, no?' the celebrant jokes. 'Makes the paperwork a little easier, right? Sorry, please continue, Bailey. If you will, your answer?'

I look at Angel with all the love I can muster. His therapy and rehabilitation have been a long slog over the last year, but he is almost back to his normal self. A deep scar still runs to his square jaw-line, but to me, he is still the same old handsome man. My lips curve into a smile that cannot be contained.

'I do,' I respond.

'And do you, Emmett Wade Michaels, take Bailey Reagan Michaels to be your lawful wedded wife?' We both look expectantly at Emmett. There is the briefest of seconds that I hold my breath, waiting for the words I have so longed to hear leave those soft, kissable lips of his. His full blown grin tells me my patience will be rewarded.

'I do.'

We do not even hear the celebrant say he may kiss the bride. Our lips have already connected, drawn together to become one. There only ever was one man for me, and only ever will be. As we lose ourselves to each other with the sun shining brilliantly behind us, I know that we are finally going to be okay.

I know I should never have fallen in love with a man who was intended to be a brother figure, but my heart had absolutely no say in the matter. Angel ruined me for any other man and being with him is exactly where I'm supposed to be in the world.

THE END